# A

# FATALITY

# IN

# SPAIN

(A Year in Europe—Book 4)

BLAKE PIERCE

## Blake Pierce

Blake Pierce is the USA Today bestselling author of the RILEY PAGE mystery series, which includes seventeen books. Blake Pierce is also the author of the MACKENZIE WHITE mystery series, comprising fourteen books; of the AVERY BLACK mystery series, comprising six books; of the KERI LOCKE mystery series, comprising five books; of the MAKING OF RILEY PAIGE mystery series, comprising six books; of the KATE WISE mystery series, comprising seven books; of the CHLOE FINE psychological suspense mystery, comprising six books; of the JESSE HUNT psychological suspense thriller series, comprising nineteen books; of the AU PAIR psychological suspense thriller series, comprising three books; of the ZOE PRIME mystery series, comprising six books; of the ADELE SHARP mystery series, comprising thirteen books, of the EUROPEAN VOYAGE cozy mystery series, comprising six books (and counting); of the new LAURA FROST FBI suspense thriller, comprising four books (and counting); of the new ELLA DARK FBI suspense thriller, comprising six books (and counting); of the A YEAR IN EUROPE cozy mystery series, comprising nine books, of the AVA GOLD mystery series, comprising three books (and counting); and of the RACHEL GIFT mystery series, comprising three books (and counting).

An avid reader and lifelong fan of the mystery and thriller genres, Blake loves to hear from you, so please feel free to visit www.blakepierceauthor.com to learn more and stay in touch.

ALREADY MISSING (Book #4)
ALREADY DEAD (Book #5)

**EUROPEAN VOYAGE COZY MYSTERY SERIES**
MURDER (AND BAKLAVA) (Book #1)
DEATH (AND APPLE STRUDEL) (Book #2)
CRIME (AND LAGER) (Book #3)
MISFORTUNE (AND GOUDA) (Book #4)
CALAMITY (AND A DANISH) (Book #5)
MAYHEM (AND HERRING) (Book #6)

**ADELE SHARP MYSTERY SERIES**
LEFT TO DIE (Book #1)
LEFT TO RUN (Book #2)
LEFT TO HIDE (Book #3)
LEFT TO KILL (Book #4)
LEFT TO MURDER (Book #5)
LEFT TO ENVY (Book #6)
LEFT TO LAPSE (Book #7)
LEFT TO VANISH (Book #8)
LEFT TO HUNT (Book #9)
LEFT TO FEAR (Book #10)
LEFT TO PREY (Book #11)
LEFT TO LURE (Book #12)
LEFT TO CRAVE (Book #13)

**THE AU PAIR SERIES**
ALMOST GONE (Book#1)
ALMOST LOST (Book #2)
ALMOST DEAD (Book #3)

**ZOE PRIME MYSTERY SERIES**
FACE OF DEATH (Book#1)
FACE OF MURDER (Book #2)
FACE OF FEAR (Book #3)
FACE OF MADNESS (Book #4)
FACE OF FURY (Book #5)
FACE OF DARKNESS (Book #6)

**A JESSIE HUNT PSYCHOLOGICAL SUSPENSE SERIES**
THE PERFECT WIFE (Book #1)
THE PERFECT BLOCK (Book #2)
THE PERFECT HOUSE (Book #3)
THE PERFECT SMILE (Book #4)
THE PERFECT LIE (Book #5)
THE PERFECT LOOK (Book #6)
THE PERFECT AFFAIR (Book #7)
THE PERFECT ALIBI (Book #8)
THE PERFECT NEIGHBOR (Book #9)
THE PERFECT DISGUISE (Book #10)
THE PERFECT SECRET (Book #11)
THE PERFECT FAÇADE (Book #12)
THE PERFECT IMPRESSION (Book #13)
THE PERFECT DECEIT (Book #14)
THE PERFECT MISTRESS (Book #15)
THE PERFECT IMAGE (Book #16)
THE PERFECT VEIL (Book #17)
THE PERFECT INDISCRETION (Book #18)
THE PERFECT RUMOR (Book #19)

**CHLOE FINE PSYCHOLOGICAL SUSPENSE SERIES**
NEXT DOOR (Book #1)
A NEIGHBOR'S LIE (Book #2)
CUL DE SAC (Book #3)
SILENT NEIGHBOR (Book #4)
HOMECOMING (Book #5)
TINTED WINDOWS (Book #6)

**KATE WISE MYSTERY SERIES**
IF SHE KNEW (Book #1)
IF SHE SAW (Book #2)
IF SHE RAN (Book #3)
IF SHE HID (Book #4)
IF SHE FLED (Book #5)
IF SHE FEARED (Book #6)
IF SHE HEARD (Book #7)

## THE MAKING OF RILEY PAIGE SERIES

WATCHING (Book #1)
WAITING (Book #2)
LURING (Book #3)
TAKING (Book #4)
STALKING (Book #5)
KILLING (Book #6)

## RILEY PAIGE MYSTERY SERIES

ONCE GONE (Book #1)
ONCE TAKEN (Book #2)
ONCE CRAVED (Book #3)
ONCE LURED (Book #4)
ONCE HUNTED (Book #5)
ONCE PINED (Book #6)
ONCE FORSAKEN (Book #7)
ONCE COLD (Book #8)
ONCE STALKED (Book #9)
ONCE LOST (Book #10)
ONCE BURIED (Book #11)
ONCE BOUND (Book #12)
ONCE TRAPPED (Book #13)
ONCE DORMANT (Book #14)
ONCE SHUNNED (Book #15)
ONCE MISSED (Book #16)
ONCE CHOSEN (Book #17)

## MACKENZIE WHITE MYSTERY SERIES

BEFORE HE KILLS (Book #1)
BEFORE HE SEES (Book #2)
BEFORE HE COVETS (Book #3)
BEFORE HE TAKES (Book #4)
BEFORE HE NEEDS (Book #5)
BEFORE HE FEELS (Book #6)
BEFORE HE SINS (Book #7)
BEFORE HE HUNTS (Book #8)
BEFORE HE PREYS (Book #9)

BEFORE HE LONGS (Book #10)
BEFORE HE LAPSES (Book #11)
BEFORE HE ENVIES (Book #12)
BEFORE HE STALKS (Book #13)
BEFORE HE HARMS (Book #14)

**AVERY BLACK MYSTERY SERIES**
CAUSE TO KILL (Book #1)
CAUSE TO RUN (Book #2)
CAUSE TO HIDE (Book #3)
CAUSE TO FEAR (Book #4)
CAUSE TO SAVE (Book #5)
CAUSE TO DREAD (Book #6)

**KERI LOCKE MYSTERY SERIES**
A TRACE OF DEATH (Book #1)
A TRACE OF MURDER (Book #2)
A TRACE OF VICE (Book #3)
A TRACE OF CRIME (Book #4)
A TRACE OF HOPE (Book #5)

# CHAPTER ONE

Diana St. James clutched the old Gaelic coin in her hand and looked at the words she'd written last in her itinerary book: *On this trip, you must do something that scares you at least once a day.*

What she was about to do in Barcelona? That *definitely* counted.

She'd been thinking about fate, about things that were just meant to be, since before the Eurorail train reached Zurich. Now, on her way to Barcelona, she couldn't help wondering if something meant-to-be would be waiting for her in the train station.

After all, sometimes, the things that came easiest to her, the ones that just fell in her lap, wound up being the most precious. The most welcome. Just like Stephane, the beautiful exchange student she'd met, all those years ago, and the lost love of her life. It was like they were drawn to her, because they simply fit. They were the things that altered her life in the best of ways.

Touching the octagonal sides of the coin, she wondered if this was one of those things. She'd been ruing not following Stephane to Paris for twenty years.

So, if this was meant to be, it was her duty to see it through. No regrets. Not anymore.

Yawning, she peered out at the Spanish countryside, awash in moonlight. The dark outlines of mountains rose in the distance, black against the velvet blue sky. Occasionally, there was a light from a village, but the sparseness of them told her that Barcelona was still far away.

She looked at the messages she'd exchanged with Sean:

*Sean: I'm waiting in the station for you.* ☺

*Diana: Sorry! I think the train will be late. We were delayed in Zurich.*

*Sean: No worries. I'll get a beer.*

That had been over an hour ago. She could just imagine her handsome Irish friend, who she'd only met on two occasions, waiting for her. It seemed like such an imposition for someone she barely knew.

She typed in: *I am so sorry. Still nowhere near Barcelona. ☹ Feel free to go back to your hotel. We can meet up tomorrow.*

Since she couldn't see much, she imagined Don Quixote charging at windmills, Sancho Panza at his side. Then she leaned her head against the window and closed her eyes.

It was nearly half past eight. There'd been the delay in Zurich, and then another delay at some town on the Spanish border, and now the train that was supposed to get to Barcelona by eight was still powering through Spain, on its way to the station. She'd had three cups of coffee, but she was still dragging. If she were back home in New York, she'd be in her pajamas right now, curling up on her sofa with a cup of tea and a good book, ready for bed.

Diana pulled her eyes open. That was one thing she'd learned during her time traveling solo through Europe—she had no one else to rely upon. No one to wake her if she fell asleep and missed her stop. And the last thing she wanted to do was wind up in some strange town on the Spanish coast, far away from her destination.

That made her miss her ex-husband, Evan. Not that he was much of a world-traveler—well, he hadn't been until he'd met his young fiancé, Tilda, anyway. Maybe what she missed most was a male companion. Someone to see to her, make sure she was taken care of.

Someone to love her.

She groaned. If being with Evan had taught her anything, it was that love was nice, but it never existed on its own. It always came with complications. So many complications, it almost made a person wonder if it was worth the security of having someone to shake you awake at your stop.

That's why, though her heart had fluttered girlishly when she'd gotten the invitation to meet Sean in Barcelona, she'd immediately tamped down any fantasies of moonlit walks and second weddings. It would be fun. Two friends, touring the town together. No expectations.

Then she looked down at her phone and saw a message from Sean: *How can I go one more night without seeing you?*

The flutters returned.

A moment later, he added to the message. *I'll meet you at the statue of the giant cat. Whenever you arrive, love, is fine by me.*

She stared at the message, now willing the train to go faster. So if she got there at midnight, he'd still be waiting for her? The horror. She dreaded the thought of arriving in Spain, only to have to go right to bed. She wanted to explore. Suddenly, she felt wide awake.

Grabbing her phone, she looked up *Giant Cat Barcelona.* The last thing she wanted to do was get lost, at night, in a strange city. Sean was so nonchalant about these sights, because he'd seen it all before. He'd left his hometown of Ballygangargin a month ago, and had been tooling around Europe, ever since. All of these places were so new to Diana, who'd never been anywhere until a month ago.

The first thing that popped up was the statue of a great lion, at the base of the Christopher Columbus statue, in the city center. Her GPS told her it was only a fifteen-minute cab ride from Barcelona-Sants, the train station.

*Giant cat? Cute, Sean. Very cute.* But that was Irishmen, for you. They had such a unique outlook on things.

Eventually the single, distant lights became numerous, brighter, and closer, and the traffic on the streets increased. The small village homes gave way to tightly packed, modern high-rises, and the narrow dirt roads became paved thoroughfares. A moment later, the wheels of the train began to squeal to a halt.

Barcelona! She was finally here!

The bright lights inside the train blinked on, momentarily blinding her. Taking a moment to text Lily and Bea, her daughters, that she'd finally arrived, she listened to the garbled announcement of the arrival over the loudspeaker.

Then she pulled out a compact and checked her reflection. Her dishwater blonde hair was still neat and styled in a springy, swingy bob, and though some of her make-up had disappeared, her face didn't carry the marks of the exhaustion she felt—no sagging, puffy undereye circles or deep wrinkles. She ran her berry-colored lipstick over her lips, blotted with a tissue, and smiled to make sure she had nothing on her teeth. *Fifty-four, and not all that bad, Diana,* she thought.

She grabbed her small travel bag and went through it. Passport? Check. Wallet? Check. Phone? Check. Itinerary? Check.

All the necessities. With those, she could go anywhere. She was ready.

She headed down the aisle, and out onto the concourse. Then she stood there, staring at the signs. *I took a year of Spanish in grade school before I settled on French,* she thought, looking both ways at all the people, heading purposefully toward their destination. *But darned if I can remember a single word of it.*

*Sí.*

There. That was a start.

It didn't matter. She'd had the same worries in France, Italy, and Austria. She'd been absolutely terrified when she'd stepped off the plane at Charles de Gaulle. But she'd made her way. If she'd learned anything over the past couple of months, it was that she might get a little lost, veer off course, but eventually, things did work out.

The good thing about every train station she'd been to was that they operated on the understanding that people might not speak the language. This station was no exception—there was a sign that said TAXI, with a big arrow. Apparently, *taxi* was the same in most languages.

The taxi line wasn't busy. Moments later, she was in a cab, heading toward the *Mirador de Colón.*

As she rode, she passed many things she'd like to see in daylight. *The Placa de España,* with its many majestic fountains and historic buildings. Two brick-façade towers stood like sentinels on either side of the street as they drove past, headed for the fountain. She wanted to find out what all the statues were for, but that would involve looking at her phone—and she didn't want to miss a thing.

Plus, as she wiped her hands on the front of her slacks, she realized something else. They were clammy.

She was nervous about her "date" with Sean.

And rightly so. Though she wasn't sure she could call it a date, really, how long had it been since she'd met up with another man, even for a casual get-together?

*Too long,* she thought. *Far too long. I'm rusty.*

Then she realized that all those places she'd wanted to explore? She'd imagined herself exploring them, *with Sean.* As she did, a little shiver shimmered through her.

*Oh, Diana. I hope you're not setting yourself up for disappointment.*

The car made its way through rather light evening traffic, toward a blue oblivion. When Diana caught sight of a large cruise ship, floating ahead, she realized that they were close to the sea. Eventually, though, it stopped at a plaza, with a large spire. She had to crane her neck to see the statue of the person atop it. " Colón?" she asked the driver, referring to the statue of Christopher Columbus.

He nodded.

"Big cat? *Gato?"* That wasn't what she was looking for. "Um . . . lion? *Leon?"*

He looked confused for a moment, but then nodded and motioned a bit forcefully, like he wanted her to leave.

*"Gracias,"* she said when she paid her fare and stepped out on the curb. The cab sped away, almost before she'd closed the door.

She heaved a breath and looked around, trying to spy the jolly man she'd had such fun with, weeks ago, in Paris. Though she'd only met him a few times, he had the kind of face that stood out, the kind you'd remember. She looked for his head of abundant, more-salt-than-pepper hair, his slightly stout, but still fit--frame, his kind, handsome, ever-smiling face. He had a good face, the face of a person you wanted to know more about. Though it was dark, there was plenty of light around the monument, which should've made spying him easy.

But she couldn't see him. She hoped he'd spy her first and come rushing to her, complimenting her on some aspect of her clothing, as he usually did, with his Irish wit and charm. He certainly wasn't shy in the least.

*I bet he's by the lion, if I can ever find that.*

She turned in a three-sixty, then took off toward the centerpiece of the plaza—the tall column with the statue of Christopher Columbus on top. She meandered toward the monument, looking around, then noticed the majestic lion at the base of the column. Its surface was dark, shining like volcanic rock under a spotlight.

There were a couple of people sitting on the steps surrounding it. As she neared its base, though, she confirmed it.

No Sean.

*Now I am totally out of ideas,* she thought, spinning. She didn't figure him for the type to play games, to tell her one thing and then do another. *Maybe he gave up and went back to the hotel.*

Awkwardness began to creep in. For late in the evening, the place was still busy. Not with people sight-seeing, though, she noticed. The square seemed filled with couples, strolling arm-in-arm.

Just like she'd imagined doing with Sean.

And here she was . . . alone, instead. *I hate this.*

She let out a little sigh. She should've been used to being alone. She'd set out on this whirlwind trip expressly to be alone. To find herself!

But every once in a while, a little tickling in her brain made her wish for something else . . .

And if she was being truthful with herself, that was what had started the trip to begin with. A memory of the man she'd been madly in love with, decades ago. Stephane, her first love, from Paris. She'd set out, all those years later, hoping against hope that she'd meet him again. Of course, when she got to the ball at Versailles, which he'd been known to attend every year, she'd been disappointed. He was nowhere to be found.

It was nothing. She wasn't foolish enough to think that, after all those years, she and Stephane would've been able to pick up where they'd left off. It was simply human nature to want connection. That's all. *Love always brings complications.* She'd do well to remember that.

Easier said than done.

She stood there, at the base of the statue, watching loving couples, walking together, whispering sweet nothings into one another's ears, for about a thousand years. At least, that's what it felt like. In reality, though, as she checked her phone, it was only nine-thirty.

Had he stood her up? Sean didn't seem like the type to be that cruel. But maybe she was wrong? She didn't really know him well. Though he was always good for an anecdote, he rarely talked about himself. She knew nothing about his family, his life . . . he could've been a Russian spy with twelve wives, for all she knew.

She checked her phone. No messages.

After a few more moments, she yawned. Yes, she should probably get over to the hotel she'd booked and call it a night.

She was just about to leave when a couple strolled by the lion. They looked up at the statue, and, a gleam in his eye, the man said, in a British accent, "Yeah, that's an impressive statue, Gladys. But I prefer the other big cat. This one's too ferocious for my blood. I prefer pussycats."

Diana blinked, as understanding dawned.

She practically tackled the man as he started to walk away. "*Other* big cat? Is there another statue in Barcelona of a cat?"

He glared at her, until she realized she had the sleeve of his tweed jacket in a death-grip. She slowly released her hold, and he said, "Yes. *El Gato de Botero.* On Rambla del Raval. *That's* the cat. This is a lion."

"You're kidding me."

He gazed at her with a look that said, *Did you fail preschool, when they talked about the different animals?* "No."

Her jaw dropped in a way that said, *Clearly, yes.* "Oh, my gosh. I just made a huge mistake."

The man slowly backed away, eyeing her as if she'd just pulled a fish out of her ear, then quickly hurried off with his spouse.

She rushed to the curb and held up her hand to hail a cab. Her years of working in New York City were good for something, because one pulled to the curb right away. She climbed inside and said, breathlessly. "The big cat! The statue? You know!"

The elderly driver nodded. "Everyone knows *El Gato de Botero.* You seem to be in a rush," he said, not unkindly.

"That's right. I misunderstood directions, and I'm late to meet someone. I thought he was talking about the lion."

"Ah. No problem. I get you there in a minute flat." He stomped on the gas, so hard that Diana got mild whiplash.

She didn't mind. Her heart raced, wanting to get there as fast as possible. After all, Sean didn't know much about *her*. She didn't want him thinking she was the type to stand people up, either.

Minutes later, the cab pulled up in front of a cheeky, fat feline, that was, indeed, a big cat. It was sitting, very plainly, on the sidewalk, about the size of an American SUV. There was nothing else around it, no fanfare whatsoever, just normal city buildings. It seemed a bit out of place, for where it was.

But even before Diana paid the fare, she saw a familiar, smiling face, in front of it. She jumped out of the cab. "Sean!"

"Hello, *macushla*," he said brightly, coming toward her with his arms outstretched. "Saw your train arrived an hour ago, and no you. Where've you been? I was about to leave. Thought I'd been stood up."

She laughed as he pulled her into a warm embrace. "Oh, well, it's a bit embarrassing. I misunderstood. I didn't know you meant *this* big cat."

He raised an eyebrow but didn't ask, something she was thankful for. She didn't want to relive it any longer than she had to. Plus, it was over and done with. She was here, with him, and she couldn't wait for whatever adventure lay ahead.

He linked an arm through hers and said, "So, Love . . . what would you like to do first?"

# CHAPTER TWO

Sean knew Barcelona well. He took Diana's carry-on bag, and despite the late hour, they strolled at a leisurely pace together, chatting like old friends who had no intention of calling it a night. The city, too, was just as alive as New York would be—people around them scurried in and out of the shops, cafés, and clubs, with clearly no plans to call it a night.

As they walked, he pointed out different sights on the way.

"That over there is Sagrada Familia, the Church of the Holy Family, Gaudi's famous creation," he said, pointing at an enormous church with four ornate spires. "And over there, you have La Pedrera. Another one of Gaudi's famous buildings. Very beautiful, yes?"

She nodded, her head spinning as she squinted to see the detail. "I'm sure it'll look better in the daylight."

"Oh. *Sí, señorita,*" he said as they stopped at a small, stucco building with hurricane shutters. "I hope you are hungry. I am so famished, I almost ate that cat statue, and that would've done a number on my constitution, I tell you. Don't think I'd be standing here, talking to you, if I had!"

He patted his stomach.

"Definitely," she said with a laugh. He always knew how to make her laugh.

They went through a narrow doorway of what looked like a private residence. But inside, there was the low rumble of conversation. The place was dark, but there was a long bar in one of the rooms, and plenty of tables packed into the small space. The hostess led them up a narrow staircase, and out into the fresh air.

"Oh, a rooftop café!" she remarked, charmed. The few tables up there were each lit only by a small votive candle.

"That's right. I've been all over Barcelona, and I'll tell you, this place has the best view in town. Good food, too."

They were led to a small table for two, at the roof's edge. Beneath them, the lights of the city sparkled. It was truly breathtaking. She sat down, and opened her menu, squinting to read it in the sparse candlelight. "So you've been to Barcelona many times before?"

He nodded. "I've been all over, in my life. Have to do a fair bit of traveling, now."

"You have to?"

She hoped he'd elaborate. Work? Play? Why was he traveling so much? She didn't want to pry, but she was interested. But he simply nodded and said, "It's a fine city."

She'd recalled him saying the same thing about Paris. Truthfully, she couldn't imagine Sean not liking any place he went to. He was so agreeable, the type of man who didn't need a party to be thrown in his honor. He brought the party with him, wherever he went.

"Well, it's my first time. How was Portugal?"

"Oh, it's Portugal. Fine city," he said, just as she expected. "Ran into a lot of foreigners along the coast, mostly Americans. They're all moving there from overseas. Cost of living is much cheaper than the States, I hear. Are you making plans to go down there in your whirlwind trip, maybe scope it out?"

She shrugged. "I don't know. Not right away, I don't think. I just got here, so my plans might change, but I think I want to go up north, after this; I think. Maybe to your neck of the woods?"

He clapped his hands. "Dublin? *Shah,* well, you should. Lots to be seen up there, for sure. And maybe I can be your guide?" He wiggled his eyebrows suggestively.

She laughed. She'd been hoping he'd say that. "We'll see."

"And I can give you insider tips, too. Like, don't kiss the Blarney Stone, if you know what's good for you."

"What do you mean?"

"The locals pee on it when it's closed to visitors."

Her eyes widened. "You're not serious."

He crossed his heart. "I've seen it with my own two eyes. It's a favorite spot for pissing contests."

She had to giggle. She'd had plenty of friends who'd bragged about doing that during their trips to the Emerald Isle. "Okay, well, I'll avoid that. And I'd definitely appreciate your help. But right now, I just want to enjoy Spain."

He nodded. "So what crazy adventures have you gotten yourself into since we last spoke?"

"Oh, it's been crazy, definitely. I saw a performance at *Musikverein* in Vienna. I went to a Shakespeare Festival in Verona. And I took in all the regular tourist traps." She left out all the murders she'd witnessed, and how, for a time, she'd been considered a suspect.

"You're a wild woman, Diana St. James," he said, and then stopped, as if realizing something. "St. James . . . do you have any plans to visit the Cathedral of Santiago de Compostela while you're in Spain? The *Botafumeiro* is a sight to see, as long as your eyes don't water up too much from the smell of the incense, eh?"

She frowned. "I hadn't . . . it's actually not even on my radar. What is it?" It certainly wasn't in any of the guidebooks and websites she'd poured over, while making her first itinerary. "Why?"

"Santiago. St. James. I thought you might visit your namesake."

"Oh! That's right. Where is it? Close by?"

He shook his head. "On the northern coast. The cathedral is there. I've always wanted to go there because I hear it's a great sight to see, but I've never made it. The *Botafumeiro* is a giant thurible, or incense burner, that they swing from the dome of the cathedral. It's supposed to be something."

She stared at him, nonplussed. "I don't . . . why do they do that?"

"Well, in the olden days, back in the medieval times, pilgrims would visit the cathedral, and they'd be unwashed and uncleaned. The incense was supposed to cleanse them, protecting against the plague," he said with a smile. "Maybe you'll get there, in your travels?"

"Maybe. Maybe you will, too." She added it to her mental list, hoping she'd remember to put it in her itinerary, later, so she wouldn't forget. It was Evan's last name, really, but she'd never even considered changing it back. It was as much a part of her, now, as her own heart. Still . . . it hadn't even been on her radar. And as much as she tried to be fly-by-the-seat-of-her-pants, the old Diana, the one who planned everything to the letter, seemed to be screaming at her to stay in her lane.

The waiter came by, and Diana was happy when he ordered a carafe of their house red. All she'd ever seen him drink, so far, was beer. She glanced at the menu and ordered the paella, simply because it was the only thing she knew by name.

He spoke in perfect Spanish to the waiter, then added, *"Pulpo a la gallega."*

The waiter nodded, and as he headed off, she leaned forward. "What did you order?"

"Spanish boiled octopus. It's delicious."

She made a face.

"It is! If you are adventurous, Diana, a right chancer, I will let you try some?"

"A right chancer?" She thought for a moment. Octopus was one of those delicacies she knew existed but was perfectly fine never sampling in her life. She'd seen calamari at Italian restaurants and always thought it looked rather nasty, with all those little coiled tentacles. But she was in Spain, and maybe a little giddy from exhaustion and the night air. So she said, "Sure. Why not?"

He grinned. "I knew you were my adventurous colleen!"

"Well, I wouldn't go that far!" she said with a laugh. "I mean, before I came over here, to Europe, I hadn't done *anything* new in ages—"

"It's time to try new things." He leaned forward, a gleam in his eye. "Which is why I wanted to offer you a proposition."

She winced, concerned by the sudden seriousness of his tone. It was totally unlike him. "You're scaring me."

The wine came. He lifted his wine glass. *"Arriba!"* She stared at him until he motioned to her with his chin. "Lift your glass."

She lifted it.

*"Abajo!"*

He put his glass down on the table, and she followed.

*"Al centro!"*

Understanding now, she reached out and they clinked glasses.

*"Al dentro!"*

She watched as he chugged the entire glass of wine and finished with a big smack of the lips. "Or as we say in my old home, *Sláinte!* Ah! Good stuff."

He poured himself another glass as she took a demure sip. She wasn't sure she could be, or wanted to be, as adventurous as he was. She'd had a hangover once, in college, after a night of too much champagne with Stephane. She still remembered the pain, the feeling of the room spinning. Still, Sean was so ebullient and fun, she couldn't help wanting to be around him. He was a magnet, drawing people to him. "About that proposition . . .?"

His face, now a bit ruddy, contorted in a question. Then his eyes brightened. "Oh, right! As I was saying . . . I'm thinking of taking a little journey tomorrow. . ."

"Journey?" Her spirits sunk. She knew he was a bit of a tumbleweed, going where the wind took him. But here, she'd hoped that she would have him around a few days, to show her the sights. Now, he was leaving . . .

"But I'll only go if you come with me."

That made her smile. That he would alter his plans, for her? "But I just got here. I haven't even had a chance to--"

"I know, but the truth of the matter is, the San Fermín festival begins tomorrow. That's when they start the Running of the Bulls, and I've always wanted to do it."

Her eyes bulged. "The Running of the . . . wait." He'd likely said something else, and she just misunderstood it because of his thick Irish brogue. "The what?"

"You know. The Running of the Bulls. In Pamplona?"

She stiffened. "That's what I thought you said." She shuddered, her body already aching at the image of being trampled by two-ton, raging animals. "You've always wanted to get gored by a bull?"

He laughed and drained his second glass of wine. "Nonsense. That doesn't happen often. And it only happens to the people in the back. The slow, stupid ones, that don't know when to get out of the way."

"But . . . Pamplona is . . ."

"Yes, it's quite a distance away, by train. The route takes three hours. We'd have to leave early."

"When is this, again?"

"Tomorrow."

Now her eyes practically popped out of their sockets and rolled across the table. "And you seriously just want us to go there, tomorrow morning? I've barely even had a chance to look around Barcelona!"

He shrugged as if it was a reasonable idea. "They have a running every day of the festival, but the first day is the best and most energetic, I hear, so I wanted to try to make a go of it."

She shook her head. She'd seen video of poor men being tossed into the air like balloons, by those large animals, white uniforms streaked with blood. It made her shudder, just to think of it. "I don't know if I'd be able to just sit there and watch you do that. It's inhumane. Bloody. Not just for you but for the bulls. I mean, what if you—"

"Not *watch* me, *macushla*. I expect you to run along with me."

She stared at him for a moment, sure he was joking. He was a lighthearted jokester, after all. But though he was smiling, his gaze was intent, suggesting that he was completely serious.

Now she began to shake her head like a swarm of bees was attacking it. "No. No. No. Absolutely not. No."

"Why not?" He held his hands out on either side of him, palms raised.

"Do women even do that? Women my age?"

"Of course! Not many, but *you* would. You're my adventurous lass, aren't you? You just agreed to eat octopus, after all. You said you came out here to do things you've never done before. I think this would qualify. Think of the stories you'd have to tell your grandchildren!"

Grandchildren. Her eldest, Lily, was due at the end of the year. She'd been looking forward to her first grandchild, but not so that she could tell it how she'd foolishly nearly killed herself, cavorting with massive, deadly bovines. "I'd actually like to survive to meet my first grandchild," she mumbled.

"Oh, you will. It's not nearly as bloody as they portray on television."

"It's not?"

"That's right. There are so many people running, and the bulls are quite tame, these days. My mate did it, years ago, said it was a bit of a disappointment, really. There are so many runners, and only six bulls. They flew by in a flash. He didn't even get close to a bull."

"He didn't?"

Sean shook his head. "Nope. Really, they've been doing it for over a century, and only a handful of people have died, and they're the silly blokes who taunt the bulls. So you just do it. See how long you last. If you throw yourself over a barrier in the first second, which I fully plan to do, so what? At least I can say I did it. I took the bull by the horns!"

She rolled her eyes at the silly pun but wound up laughing anyway. "I still think it'd be safer to be in one of those balconies, overlooking the festivities. Or here in Barcelona, which was my original plan."

"There are plenty of other things to do in Pamplona. The city has concerts, parades, dancing, and fireworks! Of course, the bull is the big draw."

He was clearly excited by the prospect, shaking his raised fists as if really taking the bull by the horns. She could just imagine him running off, being chased by an enormous animal. "You're not nervous?"

"Not in the least! I'm living my life to the fullest. And I can tell there's a chancer in you, after all. You only live once, right?"

"No."

"No?"

"You only *die* once. You live every day," she said with another sip of her wine. "And I'm not sure I want to die at the hooves and horns of a raging bull. Believe it or not, *Stampede* was not on my Europe bucket list."

"You have a bucket list?"

She reached down and showed him her itinerary. "It's not really all that full, yet. But it will be. If I don't make the mistake of *dying*."

"Ha ha!" He laughed heartily, a big belly-laugh that shook his entire body.

The only thing was, she wasn't joking.

Their meals came. As she expected, his octopus looked so . . . tentacle-y. He cut a small piece off and spooned it onto the side of her plate. She stared at it, suspiciously, poking it with her fork.

"All right . . ." He pressed his lips together, clearly a bit disappointed. "So that's a no?"

In her head, it was. But when she looked at him, she had a hard time speaking the word. Plus, she'd had all those lovely fantasies of walking about Spain with him, hand in hand. As silly as they were, she wasn't ready to give them up just yet. If she said no, she might as well have kissed them all goodbye.

Not to mention those words she'd written in her itinerary: *On this trip, you must do something that scares you at least once a day.*

Running with bulls? That would be a *big* checkmark for tomorrow.

Her mind spun with questions. Could she actually do this? "Don't you have to register way ahead of time? And would I have to wear white?"

"You wear an official Running of the Bulls outfit: white shirt and pants, a red *Faja*, or sash, tied around your waist, and a red *Pañuelo*, a bandana around your neck. I actually happen to have a couple outfits, and I think one will fit you perfectly."

She stared at him. "You planned this."

"I may have. A bit. When I decided on coming up this way to meet you, and I realized it coordinated so nicely with the Festival of San Fermin, I rented a big house in the country with all these bedrooms. You see, I've always wanted to go. It'll be a shame if I'm forced to stay in that big place, all alone."

His lips twisted and he flashed her a charming smile. She had a feeling that look had worked on many a woman before she'd come along.

Then he said, "Come on, *macushla*. Let an Irishman whisk you off to Pamplona. After we get our exercise in, we'll go out to lunch. Take in all the sights. I might even buy you a *churro*."

He winked.

She laughed. "All right," she said, so quietly it disappeared into the night breeze.

He cupped a hand around his ear and leaned in. "What's that? I thought I heard you say . . ."

"All right!" she said louder, laughing some more as she stabbed the piece of octopus with her fork and popped it in her mouth. Remarkably, it wasn't that bad. A little chewy, but with a mild flavor, similar to a scallop.

"Yes!" he said with a celebratory fist pump, then poured them each another glass of wine. "Get your running shoes on, Love! Tomorrow, we run with the bulls!"

# CHAPTER THREE

Diana yawned as the train pulled into Pamplona the following morning. She gazed out the window at the smiling faces. A festival was happening, and the mood was electric.

The sun had just been coming up, just after five in the morning, as Diana and Sean boarded the train to Pamplona from Barcelona; and though she'd hoped to get some shuteye on the train, she'd been too nervous, picturing bulls turning her into mincemeat. Also, the sights in between the cities—tiny villages, frozen in time, homes with thatched roofs and townspeople who looked like they were from another era — had kept her interested. Not to mention that Sean was an excellent conversationalist—the three hours had gone by in a blink.

Slinging one of their bags over each of his shoulders, he helped her off the train into a very busy station. The buildings in the town center were all packed together, each one, though, with its own charm— brightly colored and as pleasant as a Miami sunset, with iron balconies, most of which were occupied by people wearing white. It was clear their biggest event of the year was well underway, and the atmosphere was electric. Diana and Sean need only follow the throngs of people, heading toward the Saint Fermin festival. Mostly everyone in the busy cobblestone street was dressed in the typical white and red—even the babies. Some of the dogs were wearing red kerchiefs, too.

Diana looked down at herself, a little embarrassed. The pants were a bit large, but the sash held them up, and she'd rolled the legs into fashionable capris. Still, she'd never liked wearing white, even in the height of summer. Surrounded by everyone dressed the same way, she thought she'd blend. But she couldn't help feeling like a sore thumb, a poser, pretending to be something she wasn't.

A *chancer*, whatever that was.

Though Sean had never been to the festival, he'd clearly been to this city before, because he knew exactly where to go. He took her hand and led her through a crowd. Many of the people were already drinking beer, though it was morning. Sean helped her down a narrow alley, to what looked like a corner market.

"The Airbnb I rented was quite last-minute so I couldn't get one right on the route. So let's just leave our bags here while we run, and we'll come back for them, eh?"

*I hope there's an "after" when we run,* Diana thought, her teeth chattering.

He turned to the mustached gentleman behind the deli counter. "Hola! Enrique!"

"Sean! Buenos días!" The man came around the corner and the two embraced heartily. When they pulled apart, Enrique grinned at her, took her hand, and kissed her knuckles. "Hola, Bonita."

Diana fought the urge to roll her eyes. The two of them might have been from entirely different cultures, but they were two peas in a pod. Charmers. "Very nice to meet you, Enrique. Your little market is so cute."

"Oh, *Gracias*. Can I get you anything?"

"No. We're off to the running, but wanted to drop off our things, first!" Sean said.

"Ah, yes! And let me fill some bottles of water for you." Enrique motioned for him to put the bags behind the counter, for safekeeping, and poured a couple of small sports bottles full of water.

Once Sean dropped them in a secure location, he gave Enrique the thumbs-up. "Wish us luck!"

"Ah! *Buena suerte!*"

Diana smiled. *I'm going to need it, in a big way.*

Moments later, they were outside, following mostly young men toward the beginning of the race. No women, and definitely no old women, despite what Sean had said.

For the most part, though, it was a big festival, with lots of booths selling crafts and wares, the savory smell of cooked meat, costumed dancers, and lively music. Towering giants—people on stilts with masks over their heads, roamed through the crowd, and a band of trumpeters roamed through, playing a lively tune.

She smiled at an iron bust of a man, on the street. Someone had tied a red kerchief around its neck. "Oh, is that a statue of Ernest Hemingway?"

"That is right. He's an important man around these parts." Sean nudged her and pointed in the opposite direction. "There it is."

She looked up and saw a large, circular brick building. "That's where the race starts?"

He laughed. "That's where it *ends*. It always ends at the ring, with a bullfight. Several bullfights, throughout the afternoon. That's the third largest bullring in the world. They take their bullfighting very seriously."

"Oh. A bullfight?" She had to admit, she'd never wanted to see one of those. It seemed violent and cruel to the bull. She added, without enthusiasm, "How nice."

"It's right exciting," he said with a nod, pulling off his bandana from his neck and using it to swab the sweat from his brow. "We can get a couple beers, relax, and watch one later, if you'd like."

"I might be too exhausted from the run." *Or dead.*

He laughed. "It's a short run. Will be over before you know it."

She smiled. *Not short enough.* "Still, I don't know if I'll be able to . . ." *Survive.* "Keep up. It's that short?"

"Ah, you'll be fine. See, this is the way it goes. We line up at city hall, and a priest gives the benediction. Then they shoot off a first rocket at 8 a.m. to alert runners that the corral gate is open. A second rocket signals all six bulls have been released. That's when you need to move! The third and fourth rockets are signals that all of the herd has entered the bullring, marking the end of the event. It's very quick. Blink and you miss it, really."

She'd spent a bit of time on the train ride watching YouTube videos of people being gored by bulls on the route. Diana wagered that in the mind of someone being tossed into the air by a bull, the seconds probably seemed like hours. "Oh. Well, I'll just stay off to the side and hope I don't attract the bull's attention."

Inland, away from the sea, it was hot and dusty, and the sun was beating down upon them, with no shade except in the shadows of buildings. As Diana waved a hand in front of her face, trying to stop herself from overheating and sipping her water, she noticed a small crowd, gathered outside the arena. When she moved closer, she realized there was a man in a sparkling gold bolero jacket, red sash, and matching golden pants, signing autographs. Bright and ostentatious as a Vegas lounge singer's clothes, it was the traditional costume she'd seen, only on television. She tugged on Sean's sleeve. "Is that a matador?"

He followed her pointed finger and raised an eyebrow. "That's Alfredo De Leon. I read about him online. He's one of the local matadors, I've heard. I think he's rated highest in the city. There are a few of them, from what I've been told, that live around this area. He's probably meeting with fans."

"Really?"

Sean grinned. "Handsome, eh? They are kind of like rock stars to the Spaniards. And they get paid very well to do what they do. You want his autograph?"

She shook her head. He *was* handsome, she supposed, if she could ever consider someone who killed animals for sport, handsome. Evan had wanted to go deer hunting once, and she'd been disgusted by that, too. She had to admit, though, that there was something fascinating about the age-old custom. Just like running with bulls . . . it was a time-honored tradition, as violent and somewhat nonsensical as it was to modern people. It intrigued her.

"No, I was just interested. He's very . . . shiny."

"Yes. They are performers, after all. If he does a good job today, he'll be rewarded with an ear from the bull he kills."

"An ear? What does he do with it? Make a necklace?"

Sean laughed and shrugged, but she had to keep staring at the man, so curious was she about him and his life.

"So is that an actual job a person puts on their passport application? *Matador?*"

He shrugged, clearly amused by the question. "I don't know. To tell the truth, *macushla*, I never thought about it before. These are all good questions. Want to ask him?"

He started to walk over there, and she grabbed his arm. "Where are you going? No, don't."

"I just want to ask. I think it would be fascinating to know," he said, picking up his steady march through the crowd.

Of course, Sean would. He was confident. Unafraid in social situations. Always knew what to say and how to behave. He'd probably never had an awkward conversation in all his life. Meanwhile, behind him, Diana cowered, wishing she'd kept her mouth shut. Was Sean really going to ask the man to show him his passport?

20

When they reached the entrance to the arena, most of the crowd he'd been signing autographs for had dwindled. Now, the matador was speaking with an older man, waving his arms with a scowl on his face. It was clearly a heated conversation, because he was speaking so loudly and forcefully; it seemed to echo off the walls of the ancient buildings surrounding them.

*He's definitely got the right temperament to kill bulls,* Diana thought, freezing there. It didn't feel safe to go any nearer. *And other things, too.*

"Hey. Let's just go. He doesn't seem interested in talking to fans anymore," Diana said to Sean, trying to guide him away. "Besides, the bull running's going to start—"

"No, this might be better than the bulls," he said, intently listening to their conversation. "The running doesn't start for another fifteen minutes yet. And this is just getting good. I'd have paid extra for this kind of entertainment."

Diana listened in. *Toro, toro, toro.* Something about a bull, and a lot of no's and nevers. The matador kept shaking his fist. But that was about it. She guessed, "He . . . lost a bull? Wants a bull? Is a load of bull?"

Sean smiled at her. "No. The older man, there, owns a bull. *El Gordo*—the biggest, meanest bull in town. De Leon wants the man to let him fight it. He thinks it will seal is reputation as the best bullfighter in all of Spain. But the owner won't let him. He thinks *El Gordo* will surely kill him and doesn't want the matador's blood on his hands. Supposedly, the bull has killed every person he's come across, three so far, and injured a lot of people caring for the animal. He's a demon, the owner thinks."

"Oh," Diana said, watching them argue, red-faced, in the hot sun. A small crowd had gathered around to watch the excitement, too. Seething at one another, they got up in each other's face, so that their noses were nearly touching. Diana was sure that it would come to blows, soon, or worse. Maybe the matador would take out his weapon and slay the bull owner.

Instead, the old man backed away, spat on the dusty ground, and stomped off, muttering under his breath, *El burro sabe más que tú !* Diana knew that one from her school days: *A donkey knows more than you.* It was a favorite insult in her fifth-grade days.

21

Sean stood there, watching, thrilled by the whole exchange.

The matador was clearly in a bad mood, and probably didn't want to be asked anything. She nudged Sean. "So . . . do you think we can go *now*?"

Sean checked his wristwatch. "I suppose it's time to take our place. Too bad. I was having fun here."

"Well, we don't have to run with the bulls if you don't—"

"Oh, no. I don't want to miss the running." He took her arm and winked at her. "But good try."

"Of course not." Her teeth clenched. "What do we get if we survive?"

"Pride, love," he said with a smile, but then looked up in the direction of the matador, and his smile fell. Diana swung her head toward whatever he was looking at, just in time for the matador to stalk toward her, coming as close to her as the old man had been.

More spittle flew from his face as he ground out harsh words in Spanish. Shocked, Diana took a step back, trying to understand. "*Perra!*" he growled, wagging a finger at her.

"Uh . . . Excuse me? I don't understand . . ."

Still, the man did not relent. She tried to look at Sean, but the shiny matador was too close to allow her to look at anything other than his red face, contorted with anger. As she shrunk away, she remembered. It was first-year elementary school Spanish fodder, for sure.

*Wait. Is the matador calling me a dog?*

# CHAPTER FOUR

*"Perra! Perra!"*

He said it again and again, in a voice that didn't sound happy. No, it sounded even worse than that.

It sounded like he was *accusing* her of something. Something really terrible.

"I'm sorry, I don't speak Spanish, I don't know what you're talking about," she said softly, now marginally aware of the crowd that had been watching the other fight, swerving their attention to *her*. She tried to take another step back, but the matador was right there, intently following her, in all his shiny gold glory. He'd probably follow her all the way back to Barcelona, for all she knew.

Sean cleared his throat. "What's the meaning of this?" he said, putting a hand on the man's shoulder. He was still jovial, still the peacemaker. "Now I think you should back away. There's a good lad . . ."

The man swung his gaze to him, staring daggers, and as he did, his sequins caught the sunlight and nearly blinded Diana. She blinked, and the next thing she knew, he was pointing at her and letting out a long-winded Spanish tirade that made her head spin. She didn't even catch a single word of it. The only thing she knew was that he clearly blamed her for something.

"What is it?" she whispered to Sean, afraid to make any sudden moves. As worked up as the shiny man before her was, she couldn't put it past him to try to take her down, like one of his bulls. "What did I do?"

Sean raised an eyebrow in question and stroked the white whiskers on his chin. "It seems . . . and I may be wrong here, but this is what I'm getting . . . is that he thinks your name is Maria and that you . . . ."

"*Maria?* And what did this Maria person do? Murder his family?"

He shook his head. "I don't know. He's not making any sense." He leaned in, and with the most appeasing tone, said, *"Amigo. Ese . . . no Maria. Si?"*

Diana nodded as the man narrowed his eyes at her. She patted her chest and summoned her first-year Spanish. *"Me llama Diana. De los Estados Unidos."*

His confusion melted away. She'd hoped for a moment that his face would clear, and that he would acknowledge her mistake. Maybe shake her hand, pull her in for a hug. She even offered her hand to him.

Instead, he scowled, let out a grunt of annoyance, and pushed past her, his sequins flashing like a beacon in the sun before being swallowed up by the crowd.

*"Ooookay,"* Diana said, pulling back her unshaken hand. "What a pleasant guy. I can tell why everyone loves him and wants his autograph. If I was at the ring, I'd be on the side of the bull."

Sean shook his head. "Strange man. Very strange," he said, linking his arm through hers.

"But no matter. Come along. We have a date with some bulls."

She nodded, still a bit shaken over the whole ordeal. After that, she wasn't as concerned about the running. She doubted the bulls would be more onery than that matador.

"He's the *perro*!" a woman suddenly said, grabbing Diana's arm and yanking her away from Sean. She had dark, curly hair, tinged with more than a little gray, a long, flowing skirt, and Birks. Unlike everyone else, she wasn't wearing the customary white and red, so she stuck out even worse than Diana was worried she would. But the woman didn't seem to care. Her skin was tanned from the sun, freckled, with more than a few crinkles around her eyes.

"I'm sorry . . . who are you?" Diana began, confused until she looked down and saw the sign the woman was holding, on a giant piece of cardboard. It said: *Corridas Crueldad Hacia Los Animales!*

Suddenly, it made sense. There was a small group of people with placards, walking around outside the bullfights, shouting and shaking their fists at anyone who tried to pass by them into the arena and festival grounds. One of the other signs said, *Pamplona Se Tiñe De Sangre!* And another said, *Pamplona's Streets are Stained with Blood!*

She thrust a brochure into Diana's hand that had a similar slogan. "I'm Rachel Hawkins. I'm from Peta. I came here from America to protest these horrible crimes against animals!" she said with an anger that made Diana step back.

"Oh, I see," she said, trying to pry the woman's fingers off her arm. "You came all this way to protest the festival?"

The woman glared at her. "Of course! Of course I did! I came to band with my fellow animal lovers. This whole festival is built on the blood of these creatures, and it's shameful. The animals are scared to death, in a panic, when the guns go off. They're being marched to their deaths. It's so sad. And the bullfights? Only a coward stands over a bleeding, exhausted, dying animal and stabs him to death again and again and again—and then demands applause! People watch it—they're no better than the savages who watched the gladiators or witnessed public hangings. It's cruel. Too cruel. I can't just stand by and let it happen. Can you?"

Diana nodded. "I see . . . that's awful. But. . ." *I'm going to run with the bulls right now* didn't seem like a good thing to say, considering the wild look in the woman's eyes.

Sean laughed as he inserted himself between them. "I'm sorry, Dear, but we're late for our turn in this bloody ritual." He winked at her and led her away, leaving a scowling woman behind her.

"Sean!" she muttered, shocked. Diana's every nerve was on end now, at the intensity of the exchange. "She was kind of right. The poor animals are in a panic. Maybe we should . . ."

"Not a chance." He dragged her farther along the street. "You're roped into this just like the bulls. I'm not letting you get away, now."

Around her, people had gone back to enjoying the festival, watching the street performers and sampling the food from the stands. Diana's stomach had been doing cartwheels, even before the attack from the matador. Now, as the beginning of the run approached, it felt like it was about to roll right out of her body. She clutched it as they wove their way through the crowd, toward the starting line.

Suddenly, Sean stopped so short, she nearly ran into his shoulder blades. "Bugger all."

When he turned, she realized he was staring at his phone, a rare look of annoyance on his face. "What?"

"Looks like that Airbnb I got for our stay was double-booked. They canceled my reservation."

"Canceled?" Her heart caught in her throat. "They can't do that. Not when you—"

"They did. Sorry."

"But there's got to be some recourse to that. They can't just throw you out without at least giving you a reason. You made that booking in good faith." She motioned to his phone. "Here. Let me see. I'll call them and see what they can do."

He shook his head, pocketed his phone, and sighed. "All right, *macushla*. You got me. I forgot to put my credit card in for the ressies. And they cancelled the booking for that. It's utterly my fault."

Her jaw dropped. "You're . . . serious? We really have no place to stay in Pamplona?"

"Appears that way." He was still smiling. How could he still be smiling?

She swallowed and looked around. Something told her that finding a hotel room in this city, for their biggest event of the year, would be no easy feat. As her throat continued to tighten, she wondered if trusting Sean would go down as the biggest mistake of her life. Fighting with a shiny matador. About to be gored by bulls. No place to retreat to so she could lick her wounds, afterwards. And a travel companion who seemed to think nothing was a problem, at all. "But—"

"Don't worry, Love. We'll figure it out."

Easy for him to say. Sean wasn't prone to worrying. Or, really, to thinking much ahead about anything. She'd only known him for a short time, and already she knew he was the type who just let the wind blow him where it may, never minding much where he landed.

Meaning, the exact opposite of her.

Panic snaked its way up her spine. "How can you say that?"

"Because things always have a way of working themselves out. You'll see."

She glared at him, doubtful. At that moment, the regret was like a heavy weight on her chest. If it wasn't for Sean, she'd be traipsing around Barcelona, taking in the sights, completely oblivious to these horrors.

*Calm down, Diana. One calamity at a time. Right now, you need to think about surviving these bulls.*

It was easy to find where the race began. Police officers standing in front of city hall had formed a chain across the narrow street, barricading the runners so that they couldn't start on the course prematurely. Every iron balcony above was teeming with people. People were shouting and clapping so loudly that Diana could barely hear a thing.

"Right here. This is a good spot to start from," he said, stopping in the middle of the throng of tightly-packed bodies.

"If you're sure." Now, Diana found herself doubting his words. Maybe he had no clue, just like he'd had no clue when he made his reservations. Diana stood on her tip-toes but couldn't see much as she scanned for the bulls. "Where are the bulls coming from? Over there?"

"Yep. Right over there." He grabbed her hand. "Don't worry, *macushla*. I'll stay behind you, so you don't get a horn in your fanny."

She let out a laugh laced with worry. "I hope that doesn't happen! But you shouldn't run behind me. I'm slow. If you do, you'll definitely get one in yours."

"Ha, they say that the run is only worthwhile if you feel the breath of the bull on the back of your legs!"

The thought almost made her stomach drop out. "I swear, I'd rather it not be worthwhile, then."

He squeezed her shoulder as Diana scanned the area. She noticed the statue of a saint, and assumed that was Saint Fermin, the person the festival was named after. A loudspeaker crackled, and a man in a suit came to the podium. Smiling like a game show host, he spoke in Spanish, and everyone cheered.

"That's the mayor," Sean said in her ear. "He's wishing all of us good luck in the event."

As he spoke, Diana looked around. There were thousands of spectators behind the barricades, and security was sweeping non-runners out of the way. Shops along the route had been boarded up. This reminded her a bit of the time when she'd agreed to run in a 5k to raise money for some charity at Lily's high school. Diana wasn't athletic in the least, but her daughter had needed people to sign up, and Evan had been in surgery that weekend. During the entire three miles, she felt as if she was going to die. Twice, she'd tripped over her own feet and nearly faceplanted; and more than once, she'd nearly collapsed like a house of cards. And of course, she'd come in dead last.

Of course, that wasn't with a large mammal with lethal horns, breathing on the back of her legs.

"Uh . . . how long is the course, did you say?" she asked.

"Eight-hundred and seventy-five meters," he said, eyeing her carefully.

He was on to her, of course. Though Sean chatted with her throughout the train ride, she'd spent much of that time, studying the Running of the Bulls website, watching gorings on YouTube and learning all the ins and outs of the race. At the time, she'd been shocked to learn that it was that short a course. Not only that; the whole thing only lasted two and a half minutes. She knew that. It seemed like it would be easy.

Of course, this wasn't a running race. It was a *survival* race. A race for people with a death wish. And somehow, she'd found herself in the middle of it.

Her phone buzzed in the pocket of her white pants. She fished it out to find a text from Lily: *How's Barcelona?*

Oh, Lily would love to know about this one. That she was no longer in Barcelona, but that she'd taken a train with a man she barely knew with the goal of having a large, lethal animal chase her? Lily was her worry-wart daughter. Probably best not to get her blood pressure up, especially since she already had enough to worry about with her pregnancy.

Fingers shaking, Diana quickly typed in: *Lovely* and pocketed the phone. She'd tell them all after the fact, when she came out of it.

*If* she came out of it.

She looked around at her fellow-runners, trying to see who else was as insane as she was. Most of the women were up on the balconies, waving flags, or safely behind the barricades. She saw a few women on the street, but they were all probably about half her age. Even Sean, with his salt-and-pepper hair, was out of place. These people were all fit, spry, capable of outrunning a bull. Many of them were doing stretches, jumping up and down to get pumped for the exertion, just like they'd been doing at the 5k she ran back in the USA—moments before they all ran in front of her, leaving her at the back of the pack.

But the person in the back of the pack in that race had gotten extra cheers for trying. Here? They got a horn in the fanny.

And then there was Diana, whose feet felt like cinderblocks underneath her. In the heat of the moment, she really couldn't even put it past herself not to freeze in the middle of the street, like a puddle in January.

Was she crazy? She was fifty-four and hated running on her treadmill at home! How on Earth did she ever agree to this?

The men around her jumped up and down, ready to go. Some held rolled-up newspapers, which she'd read during her fact-finding Googling session was to taunt the bull.

*Taunt the bull? No thanks. My objective is to be as far away from the bull as possible.*

Diana thought the atmosphere was decidedly party-like, considering what was about to happen, and the danger involved. Maybe it was pure male testosterone, but even the women seemed to get into it, cheering loudly. The smell of old alcohol was a heavy cloud around her, and several of the people looked bleary, as if they'd spent the entire night prior partying.

The announcer read a benediction to patron saint of the event, Saint Fermin, and then everyone burst out into a rowdy song, hugging each other and swaying. Then, he clapped his hands and a hush fell over the crowd, full of anticipation and pent-up adrenaline.

Diana held her breath. *Oh, gosh. Here it goes.*

Sean grasped her hand tightly and squeezed it, moving her off to the side a bit. She appreciated that—in all the videos she'd seen, the bulls ran down the middle of the street, leaving the people on the edges largely unscathed. She'd leave the center to the daredevils.

He winked at her. "Ready, *macushla*?"

*No,* she thought, but nodded anyway as she watched the announcer hold up the starting gun. She couldn't breathe. She could barely see. She was going to pass out, and the race hadn't even started yet.

*BANG!*

# CHAPTER FIVE

It was like Black Friday shopping at Target, but with everyone wearing white, and no Bing Crosby's *White Christmas* being piped in.

The moment the gun went off, Diana sprang into action, running, well . . . as if a huge animal was chasing her.

Sean was still holding her hand. She'd expected he'd be way in front of her since she was no runner. But he lagged annoyingly behind, looking over his shoulder constantly, as more and more runners tore past them. Someone was screaming non-stop, like an annoying morning alarm that just wouldn't end, and it wasn't until much later that she realized it was her.

Not enough time had passed before the second gun went off, indicating the bulls were now in the street. She definitely didn't feel like she'd put enough space between herself and the corral. Again, Sean looked over his shoulder.

*What is he doing? Forward! Forward! We must go forward!* "Come on!" she cried, yanking him.

"It's all right, love! We're doing it!" He yelled, whooping loudly, as if he was having the time of his life. He wasn't running, so much as *skipping* joyously.

In fact, everyone seemed to be. The adrenaline and excitement were palpable, so thick in the air that Diana couldn't get a proper breath. Some men were squealing in glee like schoolchildren on a playground as they rushed past her. Some were laughing and a couple of women were giggling. A few of them were probably drunk. They might as well have been skipping off into a summer meadow for a picnic.

Far behind her, the joyful noise of the crowd dissolved to a low, horrified collective gasp, indicating someone had probably gotten trampled or gored. Sean started to sing, "Another One Bites the Dust."

*Be serious about this!* She wanted to warn him. *We are about to die, and you are serenading me with Queen.*

She looked back for a second, only to see Sean falling farther behind. He still had a massive smile plastered on his face, though, like he *wanted* that horn where the sun didn't shine.

"Hurry!" She screamed, arm now extended fully to keep ahold of his hand, creating a bigger gap between their bodies.

In the chaos, one of the male runners shot through that gap, wrenching her hand from Sean's. At first, Diana took it as a good thing—she could move ahead, faster. It was only a few seconds later that she realized she was doing this, alone . . . and had no one protect her from getting that horn in the fanny.

The thought made her run faster, hands on her backside for whatever protection that could give. Heart beating like it never had before, she exploded, hardly feeling her feet touching the ground as she wove her way around runners half her age. For a moment, she wondered if this was how Usain Bolt felt.

Then she saw, out of the corner of her eye, a flash of brown fur. Hot breath seared the flesh of her elbow.

*No no no no, this is not happening!*

She screamed and hung a sharp right, to the corner of the street, only to be jostled back by a man in the audience who looked like a linebacker and clearly wanted to see her die.

Right into the path of a snorting, angry-looking bull. A bull far larger than any of the other ones, she'd seen in those YouTube videos. It was like a mutant, something that could occupy its own zip code.

And it was staring straight at her.

Squealing, now, she spun around and took off like a dart. Adrenaline coursed through her veins, and she shot ahead, hearing the bull's heavy hooves on the cobblestone, mere feet away from her. She tripped over someone's leg and nearly went flying into a barricade but righted herself just in time and shot around a corner.

Above and around her, people cheered, swinging their kerchiefs in excitement. She turned for a second, just in time to see the sharp horns of the mutant bull, headed right for her . . .

"Agh!" she screeched, just as a shaggy-haired man rushed between them. The bull, not impressed, bent its head, delivering a blow to the man's butt. The tip of his horn caught in the man's white pants, dragging them down the man's hairy, skinny legs.

Even as the man began to be trampled underfoot, he flailed, squealing excitedly. Diana was pretty sure he must've been drunk, because he seemed to *enjoy* it. People applauded louder and groaned in pain as the bull had its way with the man. When it tossed him onto his stomach, he scrambled to his hands and knees and . . . began to puke, torrents of amber liquid splattering at Diana's feet on the pavement. The audience cheered. *El Gordo! El Gordo!*

*What on Earth does that mean?*

Diana managed to squeeze around him and hurry off, still looking for Sean. He was nowhere to be found, and now, it seemed that most of the crowd and bulls had gone on ahead. The noise of the crowds had definitely quieted. She slowed for a moment, breathing hard and nursing the massive stitch in her side, expecting the third gunshot to go off at any moment, signaling the end of the race.

That was when she heard a loud, feral snort behind her.

Slowly, she looked over her shoulder. The mutant bull that had just taken the pants off the puking man was standing there, sizing her up. The man's white pants were still hanging from one of his horns. It ducked its head, breathing hard, stamping the ground with its hoof.

Then it began to charge.

Somewhere faraway, the audience clapped in excitement, but that was mostly drowned out by the sound of her heartbeat.

Screaming, she turned and raced down the street, the clatter of the animal's hooves a drumbeat as fast as her own heart. Before she could get far, a hand reached out and grabbed her, guiding her to safety down an empty alleyway. She tore down it, only stopping when she heard the hooves of the bull, continuing on and thankfully, dying away.

Clutching her heart, breathing hard, she bent over, saying a prayer of thanks to Saint Fermin, whoever he was, for keeping her safe. The weeping stone walls of the narrow alley seemed to insulate her from all the sounds, providing only a distant echo of the commotion on the main street. She listened carefully, though, expecting to hear a sound.

*Where is the third rocket? Surely it's been two and a half minutes already. It feels like it's been two and a half hours! This thing has to be over by now!*

She turned toward the street. As she did, a sharp pain attacked her side. She hunched over and let out a groan. It felt like she'd been skewered by one of the bulls.

Looking down, she was surprised to find herself all in one piece.

It was just a cramp.

*Walk it off, Mom!* That's what Bea, the runner in the family, would've told her. Bea was big on proper nutrition and exercise, that is, when she wasn't drinking sake at the corner bar in Japan, where she lived. *The worst thing you can do after exercising is fall down in a heap. You have to keep moving. Get out the lactic acid!*

Pulling herself up straight and massaging her side, she walked toward the back of the alley, trying to relieve the cramp. Sure enough, Bea was right. The pain immediately started to fade, and she began to feel somewhat normal again.

*I bet even Bea, my daredevil, would've thought twice about this encounter.*

She pulled herself around a barrier and found herself on another main street, but there were no crowds around here. It was full of the remnants of celebration—empty cups and food trays, discarded red kerchiefs—but everyone had moved on.

As she scanned the area, she noticed it.

A large, shiny, golden thing, sparkling in the morning sunlight.

Something that looked like . . .

*No.* She moved closer. *It can't be.*

But the nearer she got, the more her suspicions were confirmed.

It was a body, sprawled in the very middle of the cobblestone street, on its back, staring up at the cloudless sky.

A very *shiny* body.

The matador. There was a small ring of blood on the uniform, right where the heart would be.

Her mouth moved to form a scream, but even as it did, she couldn't quite believe this was what she was seeing. When had this happened? And how?

She knew how. Or at least how it looked. He'd been gored by a bull. A matador? Didn't they have experience with this thing? Didn't they excel in swerving around the beasts, effortlessly avoiding their horns?

Well, clearly, it didn't matter. The bull had won this round.

"Help," she said half-heartedly, trying to call to mind her rudimentary Spanish. Louder, she called, "*Ayuda!*"

But the second it was out, she bit her tongue and slowly turned.

Because it turned out, she wasn't alone on the street. She'd had a strange feeling she was being watched, and she was right. There'd been another there, silently regarding her, this whole time.

Her old friend, the bull.

Her stomach plummeted to her big toes, and she thought she might be as sick as the puking, pants-less man earlier in the course. Her heart rate, which had been returning to normal, raced like an engine. She took one step backwards, her heels hitting the wall. She was trapped. No escape.

She looked up and caught sight of a street sign. *Calle de los Muertos.*

She didn't need a degree in Spanish to know what that meant: *Street of the Dead.*

And the bull seemed to know that, because it snorted louder, in a way that seemed triumphant. Its hooves clip-clopped on the cobblestones underneath as it paced about, swinging its head and enormously lethal horns, as all the while it kept its eyes on her. It seemed to be taking its time, too, enjoying making her squirm. *You thought you could succeed against me? I have you now, you puny human.*

Before she could even think of what to do next, it lowered its head and began to charge straight for her.

# CHAPTER SIX

*Well, this is a great way to die,* Diana thought as the bull began to charge for her. It was the same one she'd seen before, the mutant one who'd gored the man out of his pants. Hadn't he gone ahead? Somehow, he'd circled back on the course and was now rushing for her. For some reason, she thought she'd gone off-course, but apparently not. And clearly, the bull had missed the memo about how the race was only supposed to be two and a half minutes long, ending at the bullring.

At the last second, she jumped out of the way, but not before she heard the ripping of fabric. No pain, though. At least, she didn't think so, right then. The bull crashed into a brick wall, snorting. Quickly rounding on her, it started to come again, this time, slowly, with calculated precision.

*Oh, my gosh. Does this bull have it in for me, or what?*

The sleeve of her white shirt was hanging in tatters, but no blood. At least, not from what she could see. Is that why they wore white—to make the injuries easier to spot? She backed up until she realized she was no longer walking on cobblestones. She'd stepped on the matador's body. Actually, no, not him. His red cape.

Thinking quickly, she bent over and scooped it up. It was heavier than it looked, and unwieldy, too. Shaking it out in front of her, she contemplated the motion, even though all of her knowledge of bullfighting could be reduced to what she'd seen in an episode of Bugs Bunny, as a child. That, however, had involved an anvil, and she didn't have one handy.

So she did the only thing she could—she held the cape up, like a curtain, hoping that would confuse the bull and make him go away.

It didn't make the bull leave, but it did appear to confuse him. He stopped advancing and just stood there, eyeing her, as if trying to decide upon his next move.

Letting out a slow, measured breath, Diana held the cape up to him and began to swing it in a clumsy figure-eight, hoping to somehow hypnotize the beast. "Um . . .*Ole!*" she said, which was the only thing she could think to say. "*Hasta la vista,* baby."

The bull slowly came towards the cape, mesmerized by it. Working like the bullfighters she'd seen in the video, she slowly snatched it away and turned. The bull followed, allowing her just enough time to throw it over the bull's head.

The bull let out a monstrous growl of anger. Diana shouted as she rushed off, heading straight into an old man that smelled of cigar smoke. She tried to pull away from him and keep running, sure she was going to get that horn in the fanny, but he held her wrists tight. "*¿Cuál es el problema?*"

"What do you think! There's a giant bull after me! I think it has a vendetta against me!" she shouted frantically, looking up at the barrel-shaped man, who scanned the area behind her. He was older, and as she stared at him, familiar.

"Oh, *El Gordo,*" he said, tsking with his tongue like a mother scolding his child. "There you are. No, no, no, my big, bloodthirsty boy."

*El Gordo?* So, in other words, the giant demon bull who'd killed three people?

It was only when he released her and started walking in the direction of the bull that she realized who he was.

He was the man who'd been talking to the matador, earlier. According to Sean, he'd been the owner of the bull that the matador had wanted to fight. *El Gordo,* the meanest, biggest bull in town. The bull who apparently liked Diana almost as much as the matador had.

Now, the man was creeping slowly toward the bull, his hands out, as if trying to calm it. The bull regarded him, too, making forceful snorting noises through its nostrils, and for a few tense moments, Diana thought he might be in trouble.

But eventually, he allowed the man to reach over and grab the rope around his neck, then nudge him in the direction of the arena. By then, more people had arrived to help get the bull back on course. One said, "There he is. What happened? We'd thought we lost him!" The other said, "I didn't even know *El Gordo* was going to be on the course today!"

Prodded by the crowd of handlers, the bull stampeded off, slid around a corner on the slick cobblestones, and disappeared out of sight.

The bull's owner turned to her, a question on his face. He approached her almost as slowly as he'd approached the bull. *"¿Estás bien, mi amiga?"*

Unable to speak at first, she just nodded. Then she found her voice. "I'm fine. Thank you. But he's not."

He turned to the matador and nodded. His voice was eerily calm and controlled. *"Sí.* So I have noticed. And to think, he wasn't even running. He was supposed to be at the arena, preparing for the fight."

That was true. He was a bullfighter, not a runner. What had he been doing out here?

As she stood there, letting her breathing return to normal and trying to think of a reasonable explanation, the third gunshot finally went off.

She'd survived. Just barely. But others had not.

*

Diana watched as the police swarmed around the body of the matador. The run had ended, but rather than feeling excited that she'd survived, she felt numb. The heat was even stronger now, as the sun edged toward mid-day, but she hugged herself, shivering.

Then she noticed the giant gash in the sleeve of her shirt. She opened it and gingerly felt for any injury, then looked at it. All she saw was the slightest of scratches.

She winced as she looked back at the dead matador. Someone had thrown a sheet over his body. *Just a couple of inches, and she could've been just like . . .*

The police had taken some of the barriers used in the course and blocked off the area from curious onlookers, so the only people nearby were officials, and the man who owned the bull, whose name, she learned, was Pablo Arroyo. From her limited Spanish, she was able to understand most of what he said to police as they arrived: The victim, Alfredo De Leon, was supposed to be at the bullring, preparing for his fight with the other matadors. When *El Gordo* had broken free of the barriers and began charging the onlookers, Pablo had gone off looking for him. He'd arrived at the empty street, to find Alfredo, dead. He must've tried to subdue him, and the bull had gone crazy and charged him.

That made sense. It was nothing more than a tragic accident.

Diana let out a sigh of relief at the thought. She wasn't really sure what she would do if it was another murder. She'd been through enough murder investigations to last a lifetime.

But then again . . . being around all those murders must've aroused the suspicious side of her, because she couldn't stop thinking of the way Pablo and Alfredo had gotten into it, nearly coming to blows. If this had been deemed a murder, Pablo would make a prime suspect.

Diana shook her head, trying to clear that from her mind.

Last time, in Austria, the fact that she'd been around three murders had gotten an Interpol agent on her case. Though each time, eventually, the real culprit was found, the authorities had found it more than a little suspicious. So if *this* had been a murder, she'd be seriously worried.

*"Señora?"*

She looked up to see a young blonde woman in a ponytail. She could've passed for Bea's twin, if it weren't for the official blue uniform she was wearing. Diana paused for a beat before saying, *"Sí?"*

The woman sat down beside her, pen and paper at the ready. Diana knew this drill, but it felt much less frightening to be engaged in it with her daughter's look-alike. *"Soy Agente Carlotta Montez. ¿Cómo se llama?"*

"It's Diana," she said. "Diana St. James."

*"Americana?"* She grinned. "I have a lot of family in America. Cedar Rapids. I went to school out there."

"Really?" Though she had an accent, she even spoke like Bea. It almost put her at ease. "That's lovely. But you're from here?"

She nodded. "Oh, yes. I love Pamplona. Especially with the bulls running. It's never a dull moment! Drinking and bulls . . . let me just say, it keeps me busy! How did you find him?"

Diana smiled, at first, a bit confused and unsure of who she'd found, but then her eyes trailed to the sheet-covered body in the street. The ambulance had arrived and was slowly backing down the street. *Oh. Him.* How could she forget?

"I was in the running of the bulls. I was trying to avoid the big bull. *El Gordo,* I guess he's called? Well, I ran into a narrow alleyway and came out here. And there they were. The bull, and the dead man. I assume he must've just been attacked by the bull."

"He was already dead when you got there?"

She nodded. "At least, he looked it. I didn't have time to check."

"Hmm." The young police officer stared at her pad.

"What? It's an accident, right?"

She frowned. "Well, no. It's not that easy. It'll be considered a homicide until we determine for sure that it's the bull's fault. I mean, yes, of course, he was gored by the bull . . . we have to go through all the motions. So—" She clapped her hands. "Usually that shouldn't take long!"

This was a breath of fresh air. Diana was used to dealing with suspicious, rather difficult police who lived to cast doubt on her story. This young woman was polite and actually, a joy to work with. It made Diana miss Bea, too. "So what's the deal? What would lead you to possibly think otherwise?"

"Well," she explained, motioning to the officers as they loaded the body up onto a gurney. "Of course, being a matador is a dangerous job, but they're very used to dealing with the bulls. For him to be gored like this, and not even in the bullring, is very odd. Not to mention that he really had no business being here. *Señor* Arroyo said that he was at the bullring, preparing for this afternoon's fights. I don't know why he'd come here."

"Maybe he wanted to size up his competition?" Diana suggested, not even sure that was a thing.

The officer laughed like it was ridiculous, but then shrugged. "Maybe. Who knows? I did hear that he got into a little argument with Arroyo prior to the fight."

Diana nodded. "I was there! I think what happened was that the matador wanted to fight his bull, and Arroyo refused to let him have El Gordo, because he thought he'd get killed. They caused *quite* a commotion." She leaned in, almost forgetting this was a murder investigation. In fact, it felt like she was gossiping with an old friend.

"I hear *you* also got into a fight with him," a loud, low voice boomed.

They both swung around to look at a man that was all grizzled and wizened, like Clint Eastwood, yet not nearly as handsome. He had a scar on his cheek, running from temple to jaw, and he was almost completely bald on top, yet with bushy eyebrows that invaded his squinted eyes. He was wearing an ill-fitting brown suit that had seen better days, the knot on his tie loose.

Diana stiffened, and didn't miss the way Officer Montez straightened, too. Her voice went up an octave. "Detective Carrera. This is—"

"I know who it is," he growled, his eyes intent on her. "What I want to know is, is it true?"

Diana swallowed. "What do you—"

"Is. It. *True*?" He leaned forward more and more with each word. Now he was definitely in her personal space. She stepped back, until her head hit the brick wall behind her. "Did you get into a fight with the deceased shortly before the running took place?"

"Yes," she finally admitted.

Gathering her courage, she opened her mouth to explain the misunderstanding, but before she could, he stalked away, leaving Diana wide-eyed.

So much for a friendlier police force in Spain.

The next time Officer Montez spoke, her voice was quieter. "Forgive Carrera. He's a bit of a . . .interesting character. No family, no life besides the police. Takes the jaded detective role on a little too passionately, if you know what I mean. So you had an interaction with the deceased?" she asked, her pen poised to write.

"Well, yes. But it wasn't much of an interaction. It was really just a misunderstanding. He thought I was someone named Maria. Once he realized I wasn't the person he thought I was, he stomped off. That was all."

"Maria?" She frowned. "What did he want with this Maria?"

"I don't know. He kept calling her a dog. That's all. So clearly, it was someone he didn't like."

"So you don't know Maria?"

"No. I don't know Maria, and I'd never met him before that! I just arrived here this morning for the festival. I came from Barcelona on the first train."

"Ah." The officer scribbled something in her pad. "Were you alone?"

"No. Actually, I was with my friend, Sean . . ." She struggled to remember his last name, and realized she wasn't sure she ever knew it. "He was with me up until the bull running. I lost him in the crowd."

"Do you know where we can get in touch with this Sean?"

She gnawed on her lip. "I don't. But he's probably at the arena by now. I have his number. I can text him and ask him to meet us here?"

The officer nodded. "Please do. We'll want to ask him some questions to confirm things. And then you should be able to go on your way."

She fished out her cell phone, venturing a glance at Detective Carrera. He was staring right back at her, so she quickly averted her eyes so as not to be struck down by any of his lasers. "I wonder how he knew that I'd been speaking with the victim before, though?"

"Oh. Carrera might not be a people-person. But he's very intuitive. He knows things even before most people know them," she explained. "I know he'll probably tell you this, but you shouldn't try to leave town. Not until we have all this buttoned up. Can I have your phone number and address where you're staying, *por favor*?"

She nodded and recited her phone number. After that, reality crashed over her. The sick feeling in the pit of her gut widened. "I don't know."

"That's all right. Do you have the name of the hotel, at least?"

Diana shook her head. "You see—"

"The general location? I can help you find out the name, if you'd—"

"No. Actually, it's not a hotel. It was an Airbnb, but we didn't get a chance to stop there before the race, and then—"

"Oh. Do you have booking information?" The pretty girl's brows knitted.

"It was canceled," she said. For a blink, she imagined herself, sleeping on a park bench, somewhere. That could very well be her reality if she and Sean didn't figure something out, right away. "Overbooked. So I'm not really sure where we're staying."

The woman's eyes widened. "Ooh. That's not good. Places around here have been filled for months."

That little tidbit of information didn't help Diana feel any better. As soon as Diana absorbed the words, a bone-deep exhaustion settled over her. She wanted nothing more than to climb under a nice, fluffy comforter, settle her head against a soft pillow, and take a long *siesta*.

"I'm a suspect, aren't I?" Diana asked, her voice hollow. *Again.*

The young officer nodded reluctantly.

*Perfect.* "Am I free to go?" she asked.

The younger officer looked in the direction of Detective Carrera for a moment, before nodding. "Yes. If we need you, we'll call. But please remember what I said about staying in the area."

"Thanks," Diana said, standing and making her way toward the barricade. She had to find Sean, and quick.

# CHAPTER SEVEN

By the time Diana made it to the bullring, the crowds had thinned somewhat. People were walking about the festival booths as before, drinking beer and enjoying the music and entertainment, but occasionally, loud cheers erupted from within the ring. Diana scanned the area, wondering if Sean had gone into the ring to watch the entertainment.

Just as she was about to give up, she spotted him at an eating area, sitting in the shade of an umbrella, enjoying a beer.

She waved to him, and he waved back. "Hey, *macushla*! Think I lost you for a bit, eh?"

She slipped onto the bench across from him and fanned her face from the heat. "Yes." Then she noticed a bandage on his forehead right before his receding hairline. "What happened to you? Did a bull do that to you?"

"Ah," he mumbled, shaking his head. "No. If it had, I'd say that were some tale! It wasn't much of a story to tell my grandchildren, that's for certain. Shortly after the second rocket went off and I lost sight of you, I tripped and hit my head against a barrier. Knocked me out cold."

She gasped. "Oh! Are you okay?"

"Oh, sure, sure. Nothing that I haven't done before, after making my rounds at the pubs in Ballygangargin, ha ha!" But then he sighed. "But I cocked things up. I woke up after the whole thing was over. Like my mate, I didn't even see a single bull."

"Really?" *Well, I probably saw more than enough for the both of us.*

He polished off his beer and smacked his lips. "Can I get you a beer? Let me get you a beer. You look thirsty." Before she could argue that she probably could do better with a glass of water, since she was dehydrated from all the running, he hurried off to the nearest stand and returned with two plastic cups of the amber liquid. He set one down in front of her. "*Arriba! Abajo! Al centro! Al dentro!*"

She half-heartedly did the motions with him, and when he took a good gulp of his beer, she took a light sip. "How did *you* fare, *macushla*? Hope you at least stayed awake for the most of it?"

"Oh, yes, I—"

"Well, look at that. Your arm!" He picked up the shreds of her shirt. "Looks like you ruined your new blouse."

"Yeah, um . . . it was an adventure, to say the least . . ."

He leaned in, interested, and she opened her mouth to tell him the whole sordid tale. But as she did, a police car came screaming down the road, sirens blaring and lights flashing, and stopped at the bullring. A couple of officers, and Detective Carrera, hopped out and headed purposefully toward the bullring.

Sean watched the scene with interest. "Ah. The bell is tolling for someone. Did you hear about the excitement?"

"Excitement?" There'd been so much excitement today, she wasn't sure which of it he was referring to. Was it the bull that had stalked her, or the dead matador, or something else?

"That's right. You missed it. Turned out the big rumor is that that matador we met, earlier in the day? Alfredo De Leon? He was gored by a bull on the course. Did a good number on him. He's dead."

She sighed. Bad news traveled fast—hadn't she just left there? "You don't say."

It wasn't the reaction he'd been expecting from her, because he said, "You don't seem shocked. I know he was a bit of a blowhard, but it's still a sad thing. Not to mention, I get the feeling the police think there's foul play involved."

Now she stared at him with interest. "What makes you say that? I thought it was just an accident. I mean, yes, he was supposed to be preparing for his fight at the ring, but . . ."

"Originally, it was thought that the bull somehow escaped the barriers on its own. But now, the word on the street is that someone removed one of the barriers and coaxed the bull off course deliberately."

She wrinkled her nose. "I have a hard time believing that a bull could be lost without anyone noticing. How did it happen?"

"I asked the same question. But it turns out that there was some pretty exciting stuff going on, farther up on the course. Someone wound up on the bull's back, and rode him around a lot before he got thrown. While everyone was watching the spectacle, the other bull somehow got loose. And the consensus is that someone pushed back a barrier so that the bull could get free."

"Why would they do that?"

"Well, you heard that chap. De Leon. He wanted to fight that big, mean bull. *El Gordo.* That's the one that wound up goring him. So people think he might have let the bull loose on the course in order to challenge it. He wanted to prove he was the best. But I guess he proved the opposite, huh?"

Diana frowned. "I suppose." It was sad to think the man lost his life over something so silly, but she understood that maybe he'd been under a lot of pressure to show people he was the best. But something about it didn't sit right. A second later, she realized what it was. "But what was the good of proving that on a side street? Don't men like him usually thrive on the cheers of an audience? What is the good of beating the bull if no one was around to see it?"

He shrugged. "I don't know. Maybe he only wanted to prove it to himself."

Yes, that was probably it. She didn't understand the whole tradition of bullfighting, and she certainly didn't understand the way matadors thought. Like some people aspired to climb Mount Everest or cycle across the country for inexplicable reasons, maybe it was something De Leon had seen as his personal mission. And he'd failed. "That's sad."

Sean nodded and motioned to the arena. "There are still a number of fights going on throughout the day. Shall I try to nab us tickets?"

She shook her head. "Personally, I've had enough of bulls for a long while. And to tell you the truth, I'm pretty tired. I'm more interested in figuring out our accommodations for tonight?"

His eyes lit up and he snapped his fingers. "That's right. We're buggered there, huh?"

She blinked. Had he forgotten? She'd hoped he'd be spending this time, trying to make other arrangements. Clearly not. "What are we going to do?"

"Ah." He shrugged. "Something always comes up. The way I see it is that the good Lord always provides."

"Right," she said doubtfully. "But we should probably meet him halfway before all he provides us is a park bench."

"That is true." He stood up and polished off his second beer, then offered her his elbow. "Shall we?"

She took it. "Where are we heading to?"

"Enrique has a flat above his store. Nothing fancy, but I think it'll suit our purposes. What do you say we head over there and ask him if it's occupied? If not, he may have other ideas. But our luggage is already over there, so it'll save us that hassle."

She nodded. It was a good plan. Definitely better than park benches, that was for sure. So, crossing her fingers, she let herself be led away from the arena, through the festival, toward a possible place to stay for the night.

*

"This is going to be fine. Just fine," Sean said as he guided their luggage up a narrow staircase that was half-packed with vegetable crates.

Diana nearly slipped twice on the steep stairs, since there was no railing. She braced herself against a crumbling brick wall as she took the rest of the steps up.

Meanwhile, Enrique watched them from the bottom of the stairs. He'd been more than happy to lend them his upstairs room, saying *Mi casa es su casa,* or something. When she got to the top of the landing, he waved to her. "You two lovebirds enjoy! And let me know if I can get you anything, okay, my two best friends?"

*Lovebirds?* She smiled at him stiffly, and not for the first time, she felt like an awkward teenager, navigating her first date.

She turned to Sean as he fiddled with the key and pushed the door open. "Right. Here we are." He stepped inside. "Ah. This is great. Perfect."

She headed in behind him and looked around for the *great* and *perfect.* Unfortunately, it evaded her. What she did see was a room stocked, almost fully, with boxes and crates of food items—mostly canned goods. The place was so packed with them that they covered the windows, making the room dark. There was only a narrow passage through them, to the rest of the flat.

Diana navigated through them, following Sean. In the next room, she found a small, fifties-style kitchenette with peeling yellow wallpaper and bullet-refrigerator similar to the one Diana had seen in her grandmother's kitchen, while she was growing up. It smelled like old grease, but at least it wasn't full of crates.

Beyond the kitchenette, there was a small, pink-tiled bathroom that two people would have trouble fitting in comfortably, and a small bedroom.

*One* small bedroom.

Diana walked across a dusty hardwood floor—it only took three paces to do so—and opened another door to find a shoebox-sized closet full of empty hangers. "So . . . that's it."

"It appears so," he said with ease. "I think it's very quaint."

"Very," she said, looking at the bed. It was queen-sized, only slightly lumpy, and covered in a nice quilt, with two fluffy pillows. She would've been perfectly fine, slipping into it and sleeping until morning.

The only problem was . . . Sean.

*Don't be such a prude, Diana! It's not like you've never slept with another man before,* a voice said to her.

But her face must've given away her horror, because he cleared his throat. "Don't worry, *macushla*. I think I saw a sofa under all those crates. If I move them away, I should be able to--"

"Oh, no, I couldn't let you," she said quickly. "I mean, this is your place, your friend, and—"

"And I'm the one who dragged you out here at the last minute," he reminded her, kicking the bed.

As he did that, it seemed to spring apart a little, growing larger. Curious, he lifted the quilt to reveal two twin beds, placed together. "Ah. We could take these apart."

"Yes. That would work fine," she said with relief. "That would—"

"But we don't *have* to," he added with a wink.

She laughed, a laugh that had more nervousness than joy. Once again that giddy sensation tickled her spine, and she blushed. Suddenly aware of how alone they were, in a bedroom, she realized that she'd never been in such a predicament since Evan. "I think that we should—"

Suddenly, there was a knock on the door.

"Ah. That's probably Enrique," he said, backing out the door.

Diana followed him through the cramped apartment to find him standing in front of the door. She heard a female voice, so not Enrique. When she got there, she saw a tiny woman with a dark bob. Though the wrinkles around her eyes showed her age—she was probably at least a decade older than Diana—she was wearing a white tank-top and short-shorts, showing off a trim, fit body of someone half her age. Tanned, with bright red lips and a matching manicure, she looked worried about something, twisting her hands in front of her.

"Can I help you?" Sean asked.

"I'm looking for the American," she said, her eyes roving past him, before landing on Diana. "*Her.*"

Sean looked over his shoulder at her, astonished. Diana bristled. This had to be another mistake. Was she about to be called a *perra* again? She didn't think her heart could take it.

"I think you have the wrong person," she said.

"*No*," she said adamantly. "I know it was you. I was there. I saw you with my own two eyes. Pablo did, too."

"Pablo?" Sean asked.

"Yes. Pablo Arroyo. My husband. He owns half of the bulls in Pamplona, most of the ones used in the running."

"Ah. And what can we do for you?" Sean asked, crossing his arms, though Diana had a pretty good idea.

"Not you. I need to talk to the American."

Diana nodded at Sean, who opened the door wider. "Come in," she said.

The woman stepped inside, observing with obvious disgust the squalor around her. From the cloud of expensive perfume that wafted in upon her arrival, to her husband's profession, it was obvious that Mrs. Arroyo was used to living in far better. Sean took some of the crates and dusted them off, creating impromptu seating, and offered one to each of them.

Wrinkling her nose, Mrs. Arroyo perched on the very edge and said, "My name is Mercedes Arroyo. I have been married to Pablo for twenty years, and I know him. He cannot hurt a fly. And that is why I must come tell you—tell everyone—that he is innocent."

"And you know this because he'd your husband?" Sean said doubtfully. "You'll probably need more proof than that to convince the police."

She glared at him and spoke directly to Diana. "I do have more. But the police, they don't listen. I know for sure he could not do such a thing. He was afraid for that bull, because he'd seen what it could do."

"What can it do?"

"Oh, it's evil. It does evil things. But that stupid man. That De Leon. He did not care. I saw how silly he was, wanting to fight that bull even though my husband says no. He say no, to protect him. But did he care? No! He was stupid."

"You saw the two of them arguing?" Diana asked.

She nodded. "I was heading to the market, but I was there, by the arena, when the matador was last seen alive. And so were you."

"How did you know that was the last time he was seen alive?" Sean asked.

"They told me. They said no one else saw him, after that, until he was found dead. Several people mentioned seeing the arguments he had with my husband and you. And so naturally, we have become their prime suspects."

Diana opened her mouth to agree, but Sean scoffed. "Diana? Why, that's a textbook case of barking up the wrong tree. That wasn't an argument. Bloke just had the wrong girl. He was looking for a Maria." He nudged Diana. "Tell her."

Diana nodded. "It's true. De Leon did seem to think I was a Maria. I'd never met him before in my life. So I didn't have a reason to kill him."

"Not like your husband did," Sean added. "That fight was intense. Surprised they didn't go at it, right there."

"My husband is a saint!" the woman announced proudly. "My husband was only looking out for De Leon's best interest. Like I say to you, that bull, *El Gordo,* is not anything to mess with. He's a smart one. When he looks at you, you can tell he's trying to figure you out, to calculate how to bring you down. There's no soul in him. He's the devil itself."

Diana stared. Actually, that's exactly how it had felt, with *El Gordo.* He'd looked at her with a hatred that made her shiver, even now.

49

But Sean laughed and slapped his knee. "Come on, now. It's just a dumb bull, that's all. You make it seem like it's superhuman."

"Some people think it is," she said, her voice low, as if telling a ghost story. "It has done bad things to many people in the past. That is why Pablo hadn't wanted the bull in the running, for that reason. He was expressly against it! The mayor wanted him in there because he thought it would be good publicity. *El Gordo* has gotten his share of fame in these parts. And a bull that big and mean and terrible, in the race—people were excited to see it. To face it down and survive. But Pablo didn't want it to be there."

*That's what I did. I faced it down,* Diana thought in disbelief. *I survived El Gordo.* "But it was there. And it got free from the course."

"That's right. And the only way I could see that happening if someone let it go free. Someone who wanted it in there and wanted to cause a stir."

"Like the mayor?" Sean asked.

"No. He was at the start of the race. But maybe one of his men. You don't know how many times he begged. And always my husband say no!"

"Your husband didn't want any matador fighting *El Gordo* in the ring at all?" Diana asked.

She nodded. "The mayor told my husband that though all the six bulls in the running are usually killed in a bullfight, that day, *El Gordo* would be spared. That was the arrangement, partly because of *El Gordo's* fame, but also because Pablo didn't want any matador killed by that mad bull. But Pablo turned him down. Told him that it was too dangerous to have him in the running." She shook her head bitterly. "But he ended up in it, anyway. Somehow. I suppose my husband changed his mind. And then De Leon didn't listen. He was thick in the head. *Estúpido.*"

"You think he opened the barricade himself?" Diana asked.

She shrugged. "I don't know. But all I know is that *El Gordo* didn't get out on his own. So the police think that it was either Pablo or you."

"It's not Diana," Sean said, leaning against a crate. "She wasn't even anywhere near that bull, I'm sure."

"Uh, well, actually . . ." Diana started, to which Sean snapped his head up.

"You were?"

She nodded. "I did see *El Gordo.*" Now, he looked impressed, like he wanted to know more, but she said to Mrs. Arroyo, "And I don't think it could've been your husband. Sean and I both saw him, before the race. He was pretty adamant that the bull not be fought. Why would he do that if he wanted De Leon dead?"

"*Exactly*," she said, banging her open hand down on a crate. "That is what I try to tell them, but they don't listen to me. My husband has always been a very responsible bull owner and has treated every one as humanely as possible. He knew only bad would come of having *El Gordo* in the running this year, and he was right."

Sean was still staring at Diana, trying to figure her out. "So, macushla, exactly when did you see that bull?"

"It's a long story," she said to him with a wave of her hand.

"Ah, don't do that to me," he warned her with a wagging finger. "I want to hear it!"

"You two both ran with the bulls?" Mrs. Arroyo said, clearly impressed.

"Oh, yes. But I really don't want to talk too much about it. I'm still traumatized," Diana sighed, ignoring Sean's eyes, which were pleading for her to tell the story. "*El Gordo* stalked me, if you can believe it. Let's just leave it at that."

The woman's eyes widened. "Did it? That's *El Gordo* for you. Most bulls are dumb. They go after whatever provokes them. Not this bull. He gets one target in his sight and pursues it until the death. And he does not stop. You are very lucky. I have seen much worse."

Sean's eyes volleyed between them. "How did you survive, macushla?" Sean asked, eyebrow raised.

"Well, I, um . . . threw a matador's cape over his head, and that allowed me the time to get away. Then Pablo arrived and subdued him."

Sean nodded, now extremely impressed. Then he frowned. "Where did you come by a matador's cape?"

"Oh, it was ..." She gritted her teeth. "It belonged to De Leon. The dead man. It was just lying on the ground, next to him."

Now he just stared at her. The silence stretched on for a long time, until Mrs. Arroyo broke it.

"I just wanted to say that I don't think either you or my husband are responsible. But I don't know what to do. And I was hoping you'd have some ideas?"

Diana nodded. "Thank you. Yes. I appreciate that. If you give me your number, I'll be in touch if I hear anything."

Mrs. Arroyo reached into her pocket and pulled out a business card. "Here. Please. Whatever you hear. I'm a wreck."

"Of course."

They said goodbye to the woman, who left, her heels clicking on the steps outside. Even before the sound had faded, though, Sean turned to her. He eyed the rip in her shirt with newfound respect. "Lass, I think you need to start at the beginning and tell me just what you've been up to."

# CHAPTER EIGHT

Diana rolled over in bed, cramming the pillow over her ears.

Even so, the sound was like the loudest of foghorns, blown right into her ear. Evan had always been a bit of a snorer, but his snores had been rhythmic, almost comforting. The sound had lulled her off to sleep so often that when he was gone, she'd found she missed it.

This? This was cruel and unusual. Though he was on the other side of the room, Sean's snores were enough to shake the walls. And there was no rhythm to them, whatsoever; occasionally, it was a raucous duck's honk, then the buzz of a chainsaw, then the snort of a pig.

When she'd got done telling him a bit of the story—that she'd had a run-in with El Gordo and had been the first to find the matador's body—Sean had been full of questions. Of course. But she didn't want to think about it. She asked if they could go to sleep and sort it all out in the morning. He'd been reluctant, wanted to go out and enjoy the beautiful night, but eventually, he'd agreed. She hadn't had the energy to go out and explore Pamplona. She just wanted to sleep and forget.

But now, she was wide awake, staring at the ceiling, listening to Sean's snores, which drowned out the sound of the festival party going on in the streets below. She hadn't been able to forget anything. Though she'd barely slept at all, the previous night and her eyes felt heavy with exhaustion, she didn't think it possible that sleep would come. She never had much luck, sleeping in a strange bed.

*Next to a strange man.*

This was ridiculous. Gone were those fanciful ideas of romantically strolling through the Spanish *calles*, arm in arm, enjoying one another's company. Things like that were just that-- fantasy. Flings didn't really happen for people her age. Probably *shouldn't* happen. She was too old for that kind of nonsense. Besides, hadn't she already told herself that this kind of thinking only brought complication? Like she needed more of *that*.

Suddenly, though, she found herself in a narrow street in tow, the only sound the clomping of her footsteps along the cobblestones. The festival, it seemed, was over—the street was littered with confetti and lost red neck-scarves and used plastic cups. The banners that hung from the buildings fluttered in the breeze.

The next time Sean snored, however, there was something different about it. It was a very animal sound, and not that of a duck or a pig. "Sean, are you all—"

When she felt a hot breath on the back of her arm, she froze. She knew exactly what kind of animal it was.

Turning, she saw the bull. Somehow, it was bigger and angrier than ever, its eyes glowing red. Stamping the ground so that it shook, it let out another snort that seemed to echo around the buildings and began to charge her.

She let out a scream and spun on her heel, trying to run. But no matter how much she propelled herself down the corridor, she didn't move at all. It felt as though she was trying to trudge through molasses. And yet the bull, behind her, had no such trouble. He quickly came behind her, and she felt the point of the horn, about to dig into her fanny. She screamed.

*

Opening her eyes, Diana looked around, blinking in the light of day.

It was morning. Somehow, though she didn't quite remember when, or how, she'd managed to fall asleep.

Rolling over, she turned toward Sean's bed. It was unmade, empty.

She sat up and looked toward the door. It was open. "Sean?" she called.

No answer.

She scrambled from her bed, grabbed her clothes for the day from her bag, and went to the bathroom. Quickly showing and changing, she stepped outside to the smell of freshly brewed coffee. Sean was sitting at the kitchen table, reading the newspaper, two paper cups of coffee in front of him. "Though you could use a cuppa," he said, without lowering the newspaper.

As she slid into the chair across from him, she noticed the headline on the front. *El Matador Mata!* She winced as she squinted at the photograph on the front page of *El Gordo,* tossing the puking pants-less guy up into the air. She pointed. "That's my elbow, I think."

He lowered the paper and stared at it. "So you were there. Want to start where you left off, last night, Love?"

She sipped the bitter liquid and nodded. She hadn't said much last night, because she'd just been too tired. So they'd agreed to table the conversation until today. "I felt like that bull had it in for me. The second I dropped your hand, he was after me. He chased me into an alley, and when I came out, there was the matador. Dead." She shuddered. "The bull was there, too. But luckily the owner came by and settled him down."

She thought he'd be horrified by the story. Just telling it, she felt a little sick. But instead, he grinned. "You're not joking? That's fabulous! You really have a story to tell those grandchildren, now, don't you?"

She smiled unsurely. That, she did. Not that she would be telling anyone, right now, since it'd also made her a suspect in a murder. "It's not all that fabulous. They don't seem to know why the matador was down there. He should've been in the bullring, where we last saw him, preparing for the fight. So you heard Mrs. Arroyo last night—she thinks that somehow, I might have something to do with it."

He folded the paper carefully and tilted his head. "How could you have? You were running for your life. Same as all of us. Do they think that you moved aside the barrier?"

"I have no idea. But what I do know is that I don't think I'm going to be allowed to leave here until they've stricken me off the suspect list. And right now, I think I'm at the top of it."

He shook his head. "How can that be? They must have a thousand people who witnessed it. It was a block away from the course!"

"You would think. But I didn't see anyone when I was there. They were all a block away. At the course. The first person I saw was Arroyo, and unfortunately, as his wife said, he's also a suspect."

"It's a pickle, for sure." He clapped his hands. "*You*, a suspect. That's utter rot."

"Yes. And I'm sorry, but the police told me I can't leave the city until they have a better idea of who did this."

"They said that?"

She nodded. "So I know, if you wanted to go, you could—"

"Rubbish. Of course I'll stay with you. That's not a problem," he said jovially. "There's plenty to do around Pamplona, so let's just make the best of it. So, what would you like to do today? Explore the festival? Get some local food? Maybe take in a bullfight?"

She winced.

"No bullfight? I have always wanted to see one in person." He seemed disappointed.

"You haven't?" That surprised her. She had the feeling he had done everything.

"No . . . but it's all right, love. If you don't want to go to the bullring, I understand. Especially after what happened to you. I should imagine you wouldn't want to see another bull again."

"Well, I do think we should go to the bullring, but not for a fight."

He raised an eyebrow.

"Yes, I've seen enough bloody battles with bulls to last me a lifetime!" she said with a shudder. "Besides, De Leon was at the running for a reason. All signs point to that he shouldn't have been there because he was preparing for his fight. Something led him to the course. And I think the best people to tell us where he was headed are the last people who talked to him. Which means . . . "

"You want to talk to the other matadors who were at the ring with him."

"Right!"

He pressed his lips together. "So you're saying . . . you want to look into what happened to De Leon yourself."

She nodded. "Maybe they can tell us what he was thinking, where he was headed . . . then, if we know *why* he was on the course instead of in the ring, maybe the rest of it will make sense."

Sean let out a big sigh. "Don't you think, lass, that you should let the police handle it? You saw them yesterday, at the ring. They were swarming that place! Chances are, they've already determined why De Leon was there, what he wanted, and what happened."

"Maybe. But it couldn't hurt to talk to the other matadors, anyway." She gave him her best pleading smile. "Look, I've seen the way police can operate."

"You have?"

"Sure . . . I'm a big fan of *CSI*," she fudged, not wanting to tell him about her bad luck. He'd vowed to stay with her, and she was happy to have his help. If he knew about the other murders she was involved in, he'd likely go running for the hills before she could say "bull." "The police have a lot of cases on their hands, and they're not as invested in the outcome as someone who's been accused of the crime. Sometimes they miss things. And sometimes they come to the wrong conclusions. I just don't think I'll be able to enjoy sightseeing in Pamplona unless I've turned over these stones."

"All right, all right. Let's go to the bullring. Maybe we buy a couple tickets while we're there, though, to appease your old mate, Sean?"

She smiled. "Oh, okay. If we have to. I guess so."

"Good." He polished off his coffee. "And I'm also buying you a churro on the way."

# CHAPTER NINE

Diana nibbled on her churro as she walked, and the bullring came into view. She had to admit, she hadn't had an appetite when they set out from the room over the market, but now, as she devoured the thing, she found herself ravenous. This was no American theme park churro, like she was used to. It was absolutely delicious, crispy and sweet, with just the right doughiness. She polished off the pastry and licked the cinnamon sugar from her fingers.

"Where is everyone?" she asked as they crossed a street, checking her watch. It was after nine in the morning, so the latest running should've already taken place, and the newest fight starting shortly. But though people were walking along the various stands, the ring itself looked like a ghost town.

As they neared it, Sean pointed out a sign. He read it in Spanish and translated. "They're closed because of what happened to De Leon. No running for the rest of the festival. No bull fights either." He tsked. "Ah, what a shame."

Even though she hated the cruelty to the animals, Diana had to admit, it was sad. Bullfighting was Pamplona's claim to fame. Their bread and butter. People had probably booked for a year in advance to see these events. And now they were canceled? "No bull fights for the whole week?"

"No, it says there will be events. Just nothing involving the bulls." He snorted. "That saps all the fun right out of it. What good is the Running of the Bulls without bulls?"

As much as she cringed at the thought of *El Gordo's* breath on her skin, so close, she had to agree. It was kind of pointless to have the festival without its main attraction, like having Disney World without Mickey Mouse.

"And it says here that there is a memorial for De Leon every day at noon, so people can mourn him." He motioned to a small line of people waiting at the door. "That's probably what the line is for."

"Oh. That's nice." She scanned the area for the police cars. "You'd think the police would still be here, asking questions."

Sean frowned. "Yes, that is rather shoddy policework. Or maybe they think they've gotten all the information they're going to get from the place. And since there's no one here to talk to . . . what do you say we go on down to the *Plaza del Castillo,* sit on a park bench, take in the sights? The Procession of Giants and Bigheads is about to start and will be going past there today."

"The what?"

"Oh, it's a sight. A king and queen roam through the crowd, accompanied by pipe and *txistu* players, in their elegant dress and towering heads dancing their way through the narrow streets. They have foam batons and might bop you on the head with one of them."

She stared at him, still thinking about De Leon's death, trying to comprehend what Sean was saying. Big heads? What on Earth was he talking about? After being chased through the streets by a mad bull, the last thing she wanted was to be bopped on the head by anyone.

"You'll love it. Come on. I'll buy you another churro?"

He grabbed her arm, but she shook herself away. As much as her stomach was screaming out for another churro, she ignored the suggestion, heading instead for the nearest booth of the festival, which sold t-shirts and red scarves with bulls on them. The woman behind the counter, a slim woman in a low black dancer's bun, was handing a purchase over to a festival attendee.

Sean came up behind Diana and fingered the merchandise. "You fancy a bull shirt to replace your other one?"

Diana waved him away as the woman turned her attention to her. "Hola," she said, smiling and pointing at the booth? "Were you here, in this spot, selling t-shirts yesterday morning? *Usted . . . aquí . . . ayer mañana?*"

She nodded. "*Sí.*"

"Did you happen to see Alfredo De Leon? *Usted . . .*" She struggled to think of the word for "see," and forgot about giving it the proper conjugation. "*Ver . . .?*"

Thankfully, the woman seemed to understand. "Oh, *sí.* Yes I see De Leon. Poor man. He--" She sliced a finger violently across her neck and shook her head sadly.

"Right, right. Did you see him yesterday, before he died?"

She nodded. "Of course. He fight. With everyone. Bad mood."

"So you saw that? Was he always in a bad mood?"

"No. He *nice*! Most times. But he angry, *ayer*. He want to fight *El Gordo* and the other man wouldn't let him. So he get *roja*! And *boom*!" She gestured with her arms, miming a bomb exploding. "I stay away from him when he like that."

"I saw that, too," Diana said. "And what happened afterwards? Did you see him go toward the running of the bulls?"

"Oh, *sí*. First he go inside *el rueda*." She pointed to the ring. "He come out, few minutes later, and go right past me. Usually he say hi but not this time." She drew an imaginary line with her finger, along the path he walked, right in front of her. "Head down. Angry! I no talk to him when he like that!"

"So he was upset," Diana said pensively.

She pointed at her wrist. "He check his *reloj,* again and again, so I think he meet someone. The police say he go to *la corrida de toros.* The bulls running. But I don't know why he would. The bulls were coming to him! He was to meet plenty of bulls here, that's for sure!"

"Meet someone? Who would he meet?"

She shrugged. "He worry though. I do not trust the way he look. Like up to no good. His eyes went—" She made her dark eyes go from side to side. "Very sneaky. I do not think he go for good reason."

Sean had been looking through a rack of t-shirts that said, *Corre por tus vidas!—"Run for your lives!"* "Interesting," he said, looking up. "So you think maybe someone asked to meet him there?"

She shrugged again and turned to help another customer.

"Thank you," Diana said, whirling to look at the bullring. "I have to imagine the bullfighters are under a lot of stress before a fight. That's why he was so wound up when we saw him, and angry. Why would he just wander off from the ring?"

"That's easy. He wanted to kill *El Gordo.*"

Diana shook her head. "I don't buy that. You said that matadors are the rock stars of the bullfighting world. And rock stars aren't stars, meaning they don't perform, without an audience. Why would he have just skulked away to murder a bull in some back alley, where no one would have been able to see him do it?"

Sean tapped his chin. "That's the thing. I don't think he was thinking clearly. He was angry. If you ask me, I think he was obsessed with that bull. Kind of like Ahab and the whale. He had to kill it. And at that point, he didn't care how, or who saw it happen."

Diana's nose wrinkled. She'd like to say she didn't understand that kind of obsession, but an obsession with someone, someone she'd met decades ago, was what had gotten her in Europe to begin with.

"Maybe, but . . . I just wish . . ." She headed toward the bullring, not sure what she was hoping to do. The place was all closed off, empty. As she reached the main entrance to the ticket booth, she noticed an unassuming young man in a t-shirt and cargo pants, heading down the side alley. He had a duffle bag slung over his shoulder. She watched him as he opened a side door to the arena and disappeared inside.

Sean followed her line of sight. "Now, lass . . ."

Before he could warn her, she took off for the door. Once she reached it, she looked both ways, to make sure no one would see her. Her eyes caught Sean's. To her surprise, he didn't look like he was against it. In fact, he looked more than a little amused.

It was the push she needed to open the door. After all, she'd written it in her itinerary: *On this trip, you must do something that scares you at least once a day.*

"You're a right good chancer," he murmured as she pulled it open and stepped inside, and he followed, close behind.

As the door closed, she looked around, finding nothing more than a narrow, nondescript hallway that seemed to curve around like the perimeter of the ring.

"What're you hoping to accomplish here?"

She shrugged. "Actually, I'm not sure. But like I said, maybe one of them has an idea as to why De Leon was out at the running."

"Don't you think the police would've already asked the other matadors if they knew where he was going?"

"Yes, but it's still worth a try. Maybe if I get in the mind of a matador, it'll make sense. Right?"

"Uh . . *shah,* sure." He sounded doubtful but motioned her on. "Lead the way, Love."

She walked down the empty hallway for a few steps, until she heard the steady sound of constant exertion, as if someone was routinely jabbing at a punching bag. At the first door, she stopped to see two young boys, holding short swords. They were stabbing at a bale of hay with a bull's head. An older man, likely their teacher, was watching them very carefully. He glanced up when Diana appeared, walked over to her, and slammed the door in her face.

"Well, that was friendly," Sean said, motioning her forward. They walked a little bit farther, until they came to another door.

She pushed it open and stuck her head in, just in time to run up against a wall of hot, humid air and a sea of naked male flesh. She quickly pulled the door closed, but not before she caught a whiff of sweat mingling with baby powder. She gave Sean a tight smile. "Whoops. Locker room."

He laughed heartily and motioned up front. "How about those doors?"

They were double doors, with a window. Perfect, that meant there'd be no surprises. She crept up to them and peered through, where she could see the opening to the bullring. She thought it would be locked, but it eased open. "I hope there are no bulls running loose out here," she said with a titter.

He laughed. "Fancy a chancer like you can handle it just fine, considering you faced up *El Gordo* and survived.*"

"Don't remind me," she muttered, heading through the doors. The floor was sand, so her feet made no noise as she walked past the stands. When she reached the ring, she heard some men, speaking, their voices echoing in what had to have been a vast space.

She found the young man she'd seen outside the ring, before, standing there, with his cape, and another man, holding a mock bull's head, on a wheel. They both looked up when she approached. The one with the mock bull began shouting at her, telling her that the ring was closed.

"I'm sorry. Hi, I'm Diana St. James. Are you a matador?" she called out to the young man, her voice echoing around the arena.

He reached over the head of the bull, which was kind of like a wheelbarrow, pulled out a bottle of water, and took a swig. "No, this is the bull dance class. It's going to be a big trend in all the gyms in New York, one day, for sure," he said, his voice heavily accented but full of attitude.

His friend snickered.

"Okay, that was rude," she mumbled under her breath as she glanced at Sean. He shrugged back. She plastered a wide grin on her face. "I just have a few questions. Can I ask them? If you don't mind?"

The young man rolled his eyes. Were all matadors total jerks? "Who are you? An American?" His eyes widened with excitement. "Wait. Are you a reporter?"

"No, I'm just—"

The excitement drained away and he shrugged. "Whatever. I don't care. Americans flock to Pamplona for these weeks and thinks they own us, can go anywhere they please. Fine. But only a few minutes. I've got to practice."

"You practice a lot?"

He glowered at her. "This isn't as simple as it looks. It's an art that takes years to master. We're artists, but our art is a deadly one."

"Oh, I didn't think it was—"

"We practice three to four hours a day. But I have more time, now, after what happened," he said, strutting over to a bench. He motioned for her to sit. She did, and Sean hovered nearby. "I'm sure you heard about it."

She nodded. "Were you friends with Señor De Leon, Señor . . ."

His eyes narrowed. "Do you not know who I am?" He threw a hand against his chest. "I am Luis Castrovilla."

Her smile faltered. She looked up at Sean, who was studying a hangnail on his thumb. He was only there to humor her, obviously—he thought the idea of coming in here and asking questions was pure folly. And maybe it was. She was completely out of her element. How could she understand the victim's motivations if she understood nothing about bullfighting at all? "Are you famous?"

He snorted and looked up at his friend in indignation. "I'm only the greatest bullfighter in all of Pamplona, for three years running!"

"Oh," Diana said, genuinely surprised. "I'm sorry. I'm not very familiar with bullfighting. You look so young."

He gave an ambivalent shrug. "I've been fighting for eight years. Killed four-hundred bulls in my time, or more. I lost count."

"So you were competitive with Alfredo De Leon, then? He was very good, too, right?"

He nodded and shook his head. "Yes. Oh, he was good. Very good. One of the best around. I learned all my greatest tricks from the old man. Then I became better than he ever was. But it is thanks to him." His chin fell to his chest, and his voice cracked as he added, "It's hard to believe he's gone."

Emotions tumbled inside Diana's head. She felt a little bad to have touched such an obviously sore spot in the man, because his shoulders heaved, and he seemed to be ready to sob. But other than that, this was better than anything she'd expected. A triumph, really. If anyone could get in the mind of a matador, it was this man, Luis Castrovilla. They were friends. Maybe he even knew where De Leon had been headed.

"So you saw him before he left the ring yesterday morning?"

He nodded. "Only briefly, but yes."

"Was he agitated? Did he say anything to you?"

Castrovilla said, "Yes. He seemed upset about something. I asked him what was wrong, and he said he had a score to settle. And then he ran off. I thought it was strange, because he had the first fight of the day, so normally he'd be inside, preparing. And—" He looked over at his friend. "If only I'd stopped him, he'd be alive today."

He put his face in his hands and shook his head in anguish.

"You mustn't blame yourself," Diana said. "Do you know what he could have possibly meant when he said he had a score to settle?"

"I'm not sure. I wasn't really paying attention because I was preparing for my own fight, but he'd mentioned before that he had wanted to buy a bull, a big bull, the biggest one in ages. *El Gordo.* He was going to buy it, and kill it, and for once and for all claim his title as the best fighter of a generation. That's what he wanted. But he was upset. Someone else had bought it out from under him. I'd never seen him so angry."

"Pablo Arroyo?" Diana asked.

He nodded, surprised. "That's right. The two have fought over the sale of different bulls for years now. They hate each other. So I thought the score Alfredo had to settle was with him. I thought they were going to have words. They'd fought before, in front of the ring, so I thought maybe he'd arranged to meet him somewhere, to talk to him."

Diana paused, thinking. Only one possible solution came to her mind. "Do you think it's possible Arroyo might've asked De Leon to meet him in that place, then lured *El Gordo* off the course so that the bull could attack him?"

Castrovilla nodded. "More than possible. That's what I told the police yesterday. There's no doubt in my mind that that is what happened to my dear friend."

# CHAPTER TEN

Since the bullfights for that week had been suspended, there was no chance of seeing a fight there. As they left the bullring, a walking vendor was coming by with a cart, selling churros. Diana couldn't resist when Sean offered to get her a second one of the day.

She was scarfing it down as Sean said, "So, Love. What do you say we go for a stroll towards that plaza and do some sh—"

"Where do you think that we can find Pablo Arroyo?" she asked suddenly, looking around. "I mean, if he's going around buying bulls for the fights, he's got to be pretty well-established here . . ."

"Yes, but you spoke to his wife, right? She said he was being falsely accused."

Diana gave him a sideways glance. "Don't wives always say that?" she said though a mouth full of churro. She polished it off in record time, hardly tasting it, because now she was in such a rush to free her hands so she could get some answers. The second she popped the last bit into her mouth, she wiped the sugar from her hands and grabbed her phone. She quickly typed in *Pablo Arroyo Pamplona* and found a location. Plugging it into her GPS, she smiled.

"It's within walking distance. I think this is a sign."

"A sign of what?"

"That we need to go talk to him!"

Sean stood still, even as she headed where the little GPS arrow was pointing her. "Perhaps, Lass, it isn't a sign at all. If I have to buy you another churro to keep you here, I will . . ."

She stopped and turned back to him. "If I have another churro, I will be fastened to this spot because I'll be too big to move." She grabbed his arm. "Come on. I'll buy *you* a beer."

His eyes lit up. "Now you are talking, *macushla*."

"I'll buy you *two*, if you take that ridiculous hat off," she said hopefully.

He fastened it tighter onto his head. "I think I look good in it." He posed like he was doing a photo shoot for a fashion magazine. "Besides I forgot sunscreen. It's saving my poor Irish skin."

That was true. His face was rather ruddy from the sun, his nose a bit like a stoplight. Still . . . that hat. "You look like a tourist," she groused.

"We *are* tourists, remember?"

"But we don't have to look like them!"

He shrugged. "Never minded looking like a tourist. Besides, with my fair complexion I doubt anyone would mistake me for a local."

They walked together down the cobblestone street, past booths full of interesting wares. Of course, Sean seemed to have been bitten by the shopping bug, because he stopped, every once in a while, to look at something on the way. She had to keep prodding him along like he was a toddler in a toy aisle. When the place was in sight, he stopped and picked up a hat with bull horns. "What do you think? I think this suits me."

She shook her head. "Not really. Can we . . .?"

He motioned to the woman behind the counter and handed her a few euros, then sauntered off, wearing it proudly upon his head. She hadn't been lying. It was atrocious. Now, she was a little embarrassed to be seen with him. She picked up the pace, and this time, he stayed in lockstep with her.

They reached the brick row home with sky-blue plantation shutters on the outskirts of the festival, and she rang the doorbell. At first, she expected that he wouldn't be there, considering it was mid-day, and even without the bull running, the most exciting festival of the year was still going on. So she was surprised when a few moments later, the door swung open. Arroyo's blank stare morphed to one of recognition. "Senora St. James," he said. "You have recovered from your adventure yesterday?"

She shrugged. "Have you?"

He hitched one shoulder. "Eh. *El Gordo* was very excited by the whole ordeal. It took quite a lot to calm him down afterwards."

She hadn't really thought about her old nemesis, the giant bull, except for in her nightmares. But that bull was a devil. In the United States, it would have been put to death for killing a person. Clearly, they had different rules here. "Where is he?"

"He's at the corral, where I keep all my bulls. I have over a hundred of them, you know," he said proudly. "What can I do for you?"

"Well—"

"Wait! Come in, come in! I was just about to make myself some lunch." He motioned them into the narrow home. The first thing Diana laid eyes on was a picture of a matador, cape extended, fighting a bull. That wasn't so unusual, she thought, until she stepped farther into the narrow hallway and saw a bull sculpture, almost as big as she was.

"Oh, you . . ." she was about to remark upon the bull when she noticed another one, staring at her from the living room. It was a large photograph of the Running of the Bulls. Her eyes shifted to the sofa, where there was a pillow with a photo of a bull on it. Actually, from everywhere, bull horns poked out, and bull eyes stared at her. There had to be thousands of them. "You have quite a collection."

Sean whispered under his breath, "He has quite a *madness*, is more like it."

Diana elbowed him and followed him to the kitchen, where she could smell something good cooking. "*Arroz con pollo,*" Pablo Arroyo said proudly, shoving both hands into oven mitts adorned with little cartoon images of—of course—bulls. "Would you like some?"

The churros had tasted amazing going down, but now the second one sat like a lead weight in Diana's gut. She shook her head. Sean said, "Don't mind if I do."

He filled up a plate for Sean just as Diana realized they'd never been introduced. "Oh, Mr. Arroyo. This is Sean. He's a friend of mine."

The two men shook hands. "Please. Call me Pablo," he said as they sat down together at the table. Diana sat between them as they began to dig into their heaping platefuls of chicken and rice. "So what brings you to my home? No doubt you've been questioned by the police again, eh?"

"Have they questioned you again?" Diana asked.

He nodded. "They just left my place ten minutes ago." He shook his head. "It is not looking good."

Diana wondered if the police would've been interviewing her, had she been at the address she'd given them. Perhaps the police were looking for her, now. "What do you—"

"This is delicious!" Sean said, mouth full. "Really wonderful stuff. You wouldn't have any. . ."

Diana looked over at Sean. He'd already polished off half of his plate and was holding an imaginary bottle in front of his lips, miming tossing it back.

"Ah!" Pablo went to the refrigerator and brought out a couple of *cervezas.* He handed one to Sean, who used his own bottle opener to get the cap and took a swig.

"Mmm."

"Love your hat!" Pablo said.

Sean grinned and gave Diana a smug look. "I know. Right fine hat, I said."

Glaring at him, Diana said, "So back to De Leon's death . . . What did you mean when you said it's not looking good? Did the police say something to you?"

Pablo chuckled. "My wife said she went to see you. So you know. You know that we're their prime suspects. Just because you and I are on the side of the bull that killed Alfredo."

Diana wouldn't go that far. *El Gordo* had had it in for her, chasing her around downtown Pamplona, ripping her shirt, nearly putting a horn in her fanny. Sure, she'd have liked to be on his side, but that wasn't even close to the truth. The bull had a death wish for her. "Did they ask you where you were at the time Alfredo was gored?"

He nodded. "And I told them what I tell you, now. I was in the audience. I don't need to run with the bulls—I deal with them daily. But I do enjoy watching the spectacle."

"Your wife said you didn't want *El Gordo* in the running. That he offered you an arrangement, and--"

He nodded. "And I turned it down again and again. So that is the strangest thing. I did not even know *El Gordo* was in the running until it was too late."

Diana's eyes widened. "What?"

"That's right. Like I told De Leon, I did not want anyone fighting him, which means that he would not be in the running. I told everyone, under no circumstances would he run. *El Gordo* was at the corral, like he was supposed to be. And that was where he was supposed to stay. The other bulls are let out and put in a pen so they can get riled up for the first gunshot. It can be very confusing, very chaotic, but someone had obviously let him in there with the other six bulls."

"And you didn't notice?"

"No, I wasn't there. I only found out in the audience, when I heard the whispers and yells from the crowd that *El Gordo* was on the course. I couldn't believe it at first. I was standing on the street corner, behind the barrier, watching for him to come past, thinking everyone must've been mistaken. But you don't mistake a bull that big. He was the last bull on the course, and since he was mine, and wasn't supposed to be there, I kept watching, hoping I could somehow stop him. But he never ran past. I thought that that someone must've made a mistake or drank too much. Then I saw that some of the barriers earlier in the course were already open. So I went through one, and I heard the sound of a bull running on the street off-course. I followed it." He shook his head. "And then I saw Alfredo. And . . . you. And sure enough, my bull was loose. So I rushed to get *El Gordo* under control before he could hurt you."

As Diana turned this over in his head, Sean slapped his knee and let out a loud, "Ha!" Diana stared at him as he said, "Well, *macushla*, you were really in it, weren't you? Up to your eyeballs!"

She ignored him and said, "So you didn't see anyone else in the street except Alfredo?"

He shook his head. "And you."

"Right. And the police think you might've done it because you two were yelling at each other at the bullring a few moments prior."

"Yes, that's right."

"I heard that you and Alfredo have a bit of a history that doesn't just involve *El Gordo*?"

His eyes narrowed. "Who told you that?"

"Well, I—"

"It's true." He pushed his plate away and wiped his mouth with a napkin. "We're always goading each other. I find out which bull he's interested in, I buy it so he won't get to fight it. He finds out which bull I want, he buys it first. It's healthy competition. But it's all fun."

Sean snorted. He'd cleared his plate but had thankfully stopped short of licking it. "Didn't look like he was having much fun yesterday, outside the bullring. In fact, he looked right pissed off at you."

Diana nodded and they both turned to Pablo for a response.

Instead of getting defensive, Pablo laughed loudly. "You could say that! We're always pissed off at one another. We go back and forth, back and forth. We fight all the time. But I never would have—killed him? That's crazy. In fact, I enjoyed our little competition. I'm sorry he's gone. It's going to make my job a lot less interesting."

"You told that to the police?"

He nodded. "Not that it did much good. I don't have anyone to confirm where I was, and since I was so close to the murder at the time, they're looking at me." He shrugged. "Looking at you, too. That's why my wife went to visit you. She's worried that I might be taken away from her and locked in prison. She worries a lot."

"And you don't?"

He shrugged. "I'm innocent. I have faith in God above that the truth will come out. It always does."

"And what do you think, *Señor* Arroyo, *is* the truth?"

He took a swig of his beer and his brow wrinkled. "Well, to be honest, I've been thinking a lot about it. And as revered as matadors are in these parts, there are plenty of people who think they are butchers. Who'd love to see them dead. So I think . . . maybe one of them."

Diana thought of the crowd of gatherers who'd been protesting the bullfights at the ring, yesterday. That American woman from Peta, Rachel Hawkins. Maybe it was worth talking to her. She certainly had no love for Alfredo De Leon.

"Or, there's another possibility. Maybe De Leon did it himself. To prove himself. That's it. That's the only thing I can think of," he said with a frown. "Maybe his wife would know better."

Diana's ears perked up. "He has a wife?"

He nodded. "Carolina De Leon. She's a model. Beautiful woman."

"Do you know where I could find her?"

"In the Plaza. The pink house with the white plantation shutters is theirs. You can't miss it." He leaned in and winked. "They were very ostentatious people. Showed off, if you know what I mean. All about appearances with them."

As she was trying to think of her next question, the door opened and Mrs. Arroya came through, looking flustered. She took one look at Diana and started speaking in rapid Spanish to her husband. Diana could only make out one or two of the words: *toro,* "bull", and *ayuda,* which meant "help".

71

Pablo cleared his throat and explained, "My wife is naturally upset about the police interview. She went out afterwards to clear her head. You see, they accused me of moving the barrier in the course to let *El Gordo* through, which is a crime."

"And you didn't . . ." she said.

"Of course not. Like I said, I didn't even know he was out." He stood up. "And she wants me to show you something. Can I bother you to accompany me to the corral? It's just on the other side of the street."

Diana stood up, almost too eagerly. "Of course."

He exchanged words with his wife, patted her hand, and grabbed some keys from a bull-shaped bowl in the foyer. Then he led them across the street, to a large brick building. Diana could smell the heavy stench of manure, animals, and hay as he led them through a large arched doorway. Inside, they found an enormous corral with a vaulted ceiling, as wide as a football field. Their feet crunched over the hay on the ground as he walked them past many empty stalls. Some, though, were home to bulls, and had placards with their name and information on it. Diana braced herself when Arroyo stopped in front of the stall at the very end, knowing exactly who she'd find there.

*El Gordo* seemed to anticipate her, too, because he let out a large, angry snort, and the walls of the corral shook.

Diana froze in her tracks before she got to the gate. It was constructed of heavy metal and looked sturdy, but Diana wasn't sure she trusted it. Not with that beast.

Arroyo looked amused. He crooked a finger at her. "He won't bite."

"I'm not worried about being bitten. More like gored," she said, looking over at Sean, who went ahead easily. Sure, Sean could be brave. This bull didn't have a death wish for *him*.

"That is some big bull," Sean remarked, leaning close—too close, in Diana's estimation, to the open slats of the gate. "You faced up this beast, *macushla*? Impressive!"

Right, she had faced it before. No need to be a coward now. Besides, it wasn't some devil, like Mrs. Arroyo had said. Sean was correct. It was just an animal.

She took a step forward and met the bull in its big, dead, dark eyes.

The second she did, it charged. Sean narrowly pulled back before the bull hit the gate with its full force, causing a terrific crash. Its horns locked in the gridwork, coming inches from Sean's face. He straightened.

"Some beast," he breathed, eyes wide.

But the bull's eyes were locked on Diana's. At least, she was pretty sure of that.

Shuddering, she tore her eyes away and said to Pablo, "I'm sure he was not what you wanted to show us. Was there something else?"

He nodded and held up his set of keys. "These," he said, "are the only keys to open this gate. Well, except for the ones kept in the corral owner's office, but he keeps them in a safe. I had these keys on me during the running. So I was genuinely confused as to how the bull got out. And then I saw this."

He pointed to the padlock. Sure enough, there were little scratches on it.

"Someone picked the lock," Sean observed, looking closely—but not too closely. By now, he'd learned. And the bull was still banging on the gate with his head, not hard, but slowly and rhythmically, as if trying to remind them that he was there. He snorted and stamped on the ground.

"Interesting," she said. "Who could've done that?"

"Well, as you can see," he said, pointing around. There were many openings and entrances in the brick building, for ventilation. "Anyone could've come in here. Especially before the running—people like to look at the bulls. It's chaotic. So it's likely if someone was playing with the lock, people might not have noticed."

"You showed the police that?" Diana asked.

"Yes. But they pointed out that I could've easily picked the lock myself, to make it look like someone else had done it," he said, rolling his eyes to the ceiling.

She nodded. "Thanks for showing us that, Pablo," she said, looking at Sean. "I think we should go and talk to Mrs. De Leon."

Sean saluted. "Aye-aye, skipper."

Before she turned to leave, though, she ventured one last look at the bull.

It was still staring at her with those menacing dark eyes.

# CHAPTER ELEVEN

"Can't miss that house, that's for sure."

Diana thought it might be difficult to find their house in the *Plaza del Castillo,* the largest plaza in Pamplona, with the directions from Pablo Arroyo. But when she got there, Diana realized she needn't have worried. The pink house was a monstrosity, at the very end of the plaza. With dark iron balconies and nearly four times the size of the other narrow homes surrounding the plaza, it was easy to spot.

"I think a profession change is in order," Sean said as they navigated through the crowds, toward it. "Being a matador is clearly a racket."

Diana looked at him. She'd known him to be milling about Europe for the past few months, going where the wind took him, so she'd assumed he was retired from whatever business he'd been in. "What, exactly, do you do as a profession?" she asked him.

"Sales. I'm sure I told you."

"Sales of what?"

They'd been climbing the long marble staircase to the front door, but right then, her phone buzzed with a text. It was from Lily. *Mom? I expected more than "Lovely." I know you're busy having fun but why have you been so quiet? Don't make us worry about you again!*

Oh. So much had happened since the last time she'd properly texted her family. Though they could sometimes be a little—no, a lot—overbearing, they probably had a point, now. They thought she was still sightseeing in Barcelona and had no idea she'd even gone to the bull-running in Pamplona. Not to mention, *another* murder—

She realized she was just standing there, on the steps, when Sean nudged her and said loudly and pleasantly, "Hullo! *Buenos dias!*"

She followed his line of sight up the stairs to a woman with stick-straight dark hair, hanging down her back. She looked like a cover of *Cosmopolitan,* like one of the women Diana had worked with often for the ads she supervised for Addict Cosmetics, when she was in New

York. She had killer cheekbones and flawless skin, and long legs that went on for miles. She also bore an expression of disinterest, bordering on mild disgust, that most of the models seemed to wear.

She shooed them away with a graceful, manicured hand. "No. No tourists here. Go away."

Tourists. Of course they looked like tourists, considering Sean was still wearing that embarrassing hat.

"No, we're not tourists," Diana said. "We just had some questions. About your husband."

Her eyes widened. "Oh. Are you press?"

"Uh . . ." She looked at Sean. "Yes?"

"Then come in, please." She moved to the door and pushed it open. Suddenly, she was the perfect hostess. "I am Carolina De Leon. This is the humble home I shared with my loving husband. I can't believe he is gone."

"Yes, we are so sorry for your loss," Diana offered.

"Thank you," the young vixen responded tonelessly as she slinked into the house.

The place was anything but humble. There was a zebra-print rug on the floor, and walls were painted a bright chartreuse. Everything looked expensive, though ostentatious to the extreme. There was a giant wall in the foyer with nothing but crystal figurines. Sean's eyes volleyed around the place with amusement. "Right nice place you got here. Who's your decorator?"

The woman looked around proudly. "A friend of mine. She does great work, doesn't she? Can I have my servants get you something to drink?"

Diana shook her head and looked at Sean, who of course, said, "Have any beer?" as he looked around the glittering white foyer and whistled. "Nice place."

She shrugged, said something in Spanish to a woman in a maid's outfit, and led them through the house, to a bright sunroom. Diana gazed at all the photographs on the wall. They were all of the wife, all professional shots. Several of them were *Vogue* covers. "Oh, wow. You're a model."

She nodded, bored, and fell gracefully into a chaise as she motioned to her guests to sit in the modern white chairs across from her. "I have been all over the world. I'm the spokesperson for several large brands."

She narrowed her eyes. "You haven't done your research? What publication did you say you were from?"

Diana looked at Sean, and said, "Uh, well . . ."

*"Modern Bull,"* Sean finished, coming to her rescue.

It was fitting, Diana thought. This was a lot of modern bull.

The woman's carefully shaped eyebrow quirked up. "Oh. So you are hear about Alfie. I've never heard of that publication, though."

"We have a big readership in America," Diana finished up, studying the woman. Though the death of her husband had happened barely twenty-four hours before, she was in remarkably good spirits. And she was definitely younger than De Leon—she looked as if she was in her younger twenties, and De Leon had been at least forty.

"Oh, is that so?" She finger-combed her hair. "I go to New York at least once a season, for Fashion Week. In fact, I'm supposed to leave in a couple days. I suppose I won't, though. I'm too distraught after poor Alfie."

Was she? There wasn't a sign at all that she was upset—no red eyes, running mascara. In fact, she looked as if she'd just walked off a runway. Was that natural, or did she work hard to look that perfect? "I imagine it must've been a shock to you."

*"Ay, caray!"* she shouted suddenly, looking at her fingernail with disdain. "I broke a nail."

She snapped at one of her servants, who came rushing forward with a file. As fast as they appeared with the instrument, this must've been a regular, expected occurrence.

"Like I said, my poor, poor husband." She sighed as she began to file. "It makes no sense to me. The police tell me the bull wasn't even on the course! Wasn't even supposed to be running! I don't understand. And now, here I am, a widow at twenty-two!"

Sean shook his head. "That's a terrible thing."

She looked around the house. "We'd just moved into this place. Only married six months. Most of it was our honeymoon. We had such lovely parties here. And now . . . Now I am alone."

Rather than sadness, Diana couldn't help but think she saw a little glimmer of excitement in the young woman's eyes. Carolina was young like her daughters, Bea and Lily, and yet, Diana couldn't see any resemblance whatsoever.

"I've heard some people suggest that your husband had a bit of obsession with fighting that bull. *El Gordo?"* Diana suggested gently.

The woman shook her head. "That is silly. He only had an obsession with that bull owner."

"You mean Pablo Arroyo?"

She shrugged. "I do not know his name. I do not pay much attention to my husband's affairs. Bulls, they do not interest me. But I know that Alfie and that man, they did not like each other. Always at each other's throats. Always fighting. Last time he bought *El Gordo* out from under Alfie and I never hear the end of it!"

"So you think he had something to do with it?"

"Obviously! That is what I told the police. He was not a nice man. And how else would that bull have gotten out and been off the course like that?" She shook her head. "I live in Pamplona all my life. My brothers and father and grandfather all run with bulls. My great grandfather a matador. He introduce Alfie and me. I know how it work."

"You didn't go to the running though?" Sean put in, as the maid came and gave him his *cerveza*. He took a big gulp and smacked his lips as the maid brought a fruity cocktail for the woman.

She took a sip through the straw with her perfect pink lips and shook her head. "Oh, no no. I think it too violent. It makes my stomach ill. All that blood!"

"There are a lot of people who feel that way," Diana pointed out. "That the bullfighting is too brutal a sport. Did he ever make any other enemies because of it?"

She shrugged. "Every once in a while when we go out to eat, some stupid activist come up and yell at him. One even spit on us! It was disgusting. I tell Alfie no more. He was used to it, but not me. I'm used to the paparazzi following me, snapping photos, but they're not like those awful Peta people. So he get a bodyguard for us whenever we go out together."

"Bodyguard?"

She nodded. "Yes, but he doesn't use him when he's alone. Only for me."

"Oh. So you really think Arroyo's to blame," she said thoughtfully.

Carolina nodded. "Those activists are disgusting but they are not murderers. So who else could it be?"

Diana tried to imagine the angry little man she'd seen on the street with this beautiful young woman. She supposed it was like how unattractive male rock stars always wound up nabbing beautiful models—they liked the bad boy. Because she really couldn't see these two together as a couple.

Suddenly, something occurred to her. "What about Maria?"

The woman's doe eyes widened. "Maria? I don't know any Maria."

Sean looked at her, then said, "We saw your husband shortly before the incident, and he mistook Diana here for someone named Maria. He was upset so it was clearly someone he wasn't happy with."

Carolina looked at them in confusion. "Maria? No . . . look, you two. I do not for one moment think that I was the only woman in Alfie's life. I do know he had a long line of women before me, and many were obsessed with him. Many were not happy when we married. He would get notes and letters from them, so I know."

"Any of them follow you two around, that you know of?" Sean asked.

She shook her head. "The bodyguard took care of that. And the letters and notes eventually stopped coming."

"But . . . still. It could've been an obsessed ex-lover?" Diana asked.

She shrugged. "I do not think so, though."

"Why?"

"Well, because if a woman wanted to see him dead, she'd poison him!" she said with a laugh. "She wouldn't attempt to have a two-ton beast gore him. It doesn't make sense."

Diana stared at the woman. She was smarter than Diana had been giving her credit for. Or maybe she'd just thought about murder an awful lot. Either way, a shiver ran up her spine. This was nasty business.

"All right, so we're back to square one," Sean said.

"Hold on. Señora De Leon, you say he wasn't obsessed with that bull he tried to buy. There's talk on the street he may have tried to release the bull himself, so he could fight it."

She shook her head. "Oh, no. He would not do that. In a back alley like that? You don't know Alfie if you believe that. He needed his audience. Thrived upon it. If he'd vanquished that bull without anyone knowing, what would be the point? Juan would've been so upset at him—he never would've heard the end of it."

Sean asked, "Juan?"

"Juan Perez. His manager. Juan manages all the matadors in the area."

"Do you have information for him?" she asked, ignoring the rolled eyes she was getting from Sean.

"Yes, somewhere." She snapped her finger again for her servant and spoke to them in Spanish. They scurried off for a moment, then returned with a piece of paper. Carolina inspected it before handing it over. "Ah, right. His office is located near the bullring. I never go there but he might have more information for you, for your story. Is it about his death?"

Diana nodded and stood up, a little discouraged. Everything seemed to bring her back to Arroyo. And after her discussion with him, she was pretty sure he was innocent. "Yes, we're doing a tribute. We'll send you a copy when it's done. Well, thank y--."

"Tribute? You didn't even ask for any photographs?"

"Oh. We have plenty of those. And we're also going to focus on the last days, before his death. So we just wanted to get a few quotes from you, his wife. We appreciate your time," she babbled, eyeing the door. She couldn't wait to leave.

"There is one more thing," Carolina said, and for the first time, a little wrinkle appeared on the bridge of her nose. She suddenly looked worried.

"Yes?" Diana asked, leaning forward.

"Well, I tell Alfie I don't like the bullfighting. I say to him he must give it up. And he was going to. He told me he'd retire after one last fight." She sighed. "And this was his last fight. Only, he lost. *Idiota.*"

# CHAPTER TWELVE

"Lovely girl," Sean said as they headed back down the steps, to the street.

"She *was* a bit self-absorbed," Diana remarked as she looked around, wondering where to go next. "Or were you being serious, saying she was lovely only because she was absolutely gorgeous?"

"A *bit* self-absorbed? Love, there's only room in that girl's heart for one person—herself. A woman like that would drive most men up a wall, after the initial sparkle wore off. Look!" Sean said just as Diana's eyes fastened on a large crowd, at the other side of the plaza. "Let's go."

He took her hand and led her toward the fray. People were clapping and shouting as upbeat flute music played. Diana noticed a couple of large-headed people who appeared to be on stilts, meandering through the crowd.

She stopped. Sean tried to pull her, but she stayed still. "Is this that Bighead thing you were talking about? No thanks."

"Yes! The Procession of Giants and Bigheads!" He succeeded in pulling her a little farther. Then he did a little jig. "Come on. It's fun!"

"No, thanks, Sean. I really am not in the mood to be bopped on the head."

"What happened to my chancer?"

She motioned to a café nearby. The tables outside were crowded because it was such a beautiful day, but a couple was just standing up from one of them. "How about instead, I buy you a beer?"

He didn't even blink. "Sold."

She had to laugh at him. He'd pretty much gone on drinking through this entire trip, and he had yet to even appear drunk. Well, he was normally surly and a bit off-kilter, to begin with. The beer didn't change that. She sat down with him, and this time, she ordered a beer, herself.

"*Arriba! Abajo! Al centro! Al dentro!*" she said with him, going through the motions before taking a drink.

As she sipped it, she watched the procession make its way down the center of the plaza, sure enough, the Big Heads going around and walloping laughing people on the head.

"So much fun," she said without interest as the crowd followed it out of sight down a narrow side street.

"Well, it certainly was better than marinating in that spoiled brat's company for any length of time," Sean said, hooking a thumb over his shoulder to point to the pink mansion.

"She's definitely spoiled. It's like she didn't care at all about her husband's death," Diana agreed.

"Didn't care?" He laughed, long and hard. "Of course not. She likely bumped the poor bloke off, herself."

"Hmm. I was wondering about that, too. You really think she could've done it, though? It seems an unlikely way for a woman to murder a husband."

"Yep. Money grubbing. She married him for his money and then offed him as soon as she could. And never underestimate what a gold-digging wife can do."

He was entirely serious. And, Diana reasoned, it did make sense, considering her lack of emotion. But something about it just didn't sit right. "I don't know. She seemed pretty successful on her own, with the modeling. She didn't really need his money."

He leaned back in his chair and cracked his back loudly. "For people like that, enough is never enough. I bet you anything she probably has a big life insurance payout coming to her now."

"You think?"

"Of course. Dangerous job like that, I bet he has loads of insurance on his head. But I think she was lying when she said she wasn't there. I wouldn't put it past her to follow him, open the barrier, and let the bull loose."

"I don't know. Someone like her? People would notice if she'd been on the course."

"I suppose that's true." He shrugged. "So, let me guess. You want to go see the manager."

"Would you mind?" She asked, taking out the piece of paper and reading the address aloud. "I promise, we won't be there that—"

He held up his beer. "You bought me this. It's the key to my heart. We can go wherever you like, *macushla,* and I will gladly be your escort."

She smiled. "Good, let's go!"

"But you haven't finished your—"

She was up already, heading back toward the bullring. When he caught up with her, he was holding not only his own beer, but her unfinished beer as well. She laughed at him. "Can't let a good beer go to waste, hmm?"

"Truer words were never spoken." He laughed. "But no, I brought this one for you. You have to keep your strength up."

She laughed some more and took it from him, then took a sip as they walked. Having to drink the beer slowed her down enough so that she wasn't just rushing to the next place. As they walked, she managed to stop and look at the wares at some of the booths. There was a place selling beautiful, brightly colored pottery, and another selling paintings of some of the most historic buildings in the area.

Her eyes caught on a beautiful, tiny portrait, of the hilly cobblestone street, framed by the festively colored homes with their wrought-iron balconies and ivy-covered trellises. In the background, a large cathedral rose up. She squinted to read it. *Santa María la Real.* "This one is pretty."

"You like it?" he said, nodding in agreement. He motioned to the clerk, money was exchanged, and moments later, he was carrying a bag with a smaller version of it. He handed it to her. "For you."

"Oh, you didn't have to—"

"We all need something to remember this trip by. I have this fetching hat." He pointed at the bull horned hat. "You have the painting."

She smiled and looked up at his hat as she tucked the painting into her purse. Though he looked ridiculous, she had to smile. He didn't care what anyone thought. If they were pegged as tourists, good. So was everyone else, around here. She needed to be more like him and stop worrying about what everyone else was thinking.

So she drained her beer. By the time they got to the place outside the bullring, she was a bit light-headed and feeling happy.

*I'm tipsy,* she thought, having to concentrate on putting one foot in front of the other on the uneven cobblestones.

When they stopped at the corner, she realized that though the bullfights had been cancelled, the protestors were back. Fewer of them, at least. They were sitting on the curb, silent, since there really wasn't anyone nearby to harass. It was that Rachel Hawkins, wearing a sign that said, *DE LEON'S DEATH IS A VICTORY!*

Nice.

"That's bloody brutal," Sean said, shaking his head. "They could at least give the poor bloke some respect."

Diana scanned the area and noticed a small storefront across the street from the ring. Though it looked closed-up, there was some writing on the window, in regal script, that said, *Oficina de Juan Perez, Abogado.*

She pointed. "There's his office. Let's go."

They made sure to stay on the street opposite the protestors as they made their way to the office building. Diana pushed open the door to a little jingling bell. Inside, it looked a bit like a dentist's office. "Hola!" a disembodied voice called from behind a receptionist's window.

Diana approached it and looked in to find an older woman, studying them expectantly. *"Hola,"* Diana said as the woman slid the window open, *"Me llama Diana . . . habla ingles?"*

And that was where her knowledge of Spanish ran out, so she really hoped the woman spoke English.

She nodded and said in very accented English, "What can I do for you?"

"Is this the office of the Juan Perez, who manages certain bullfighters?"

She nodded. "Yes, he does. Are you looking to secure a bullfighter for an event?"

Diana shook her head. "No. I don't have an appointment, but I was wondering if I could talk to Señor Perez? It would only take a moment?"

"What is this in relation to?"

"It's about Alfredo De Leon. I'm sure you've heard about the tragedy by now."

Her eyes widened as she took the phone's receiver in her hand. "Of course, of course. It's terrible. He was very talented. Are you . . . police?"

She shook her head. "Just friends of his."

The woman slid the window closed, dialed and spoke in a low voice to whoever was on the other end, giving her furtive glances as she did. Finally, she hung up the phone and stood up. The next moment, the door opened, and the older woman said, "Come this way."

If Juan Perez managed some of the best matadors in Spain, one wouldn't have known it from the shabby appearance of the office. The hallway was all seventies-style paneling with old paintings of yellow flowers and generic beach scenes more suitable for a hotel. There was even a typewriter and a fax machine in the corner of the cluttered hallway, piled in a heap, as if someone was a hoarder.

Diana sneezed loudly. The dust was almost overwhelming. The woman pushed open a door and motioned them through. Inside, Diana found a man in a shabby dress shirt and combover. He looked like a used car salesman. His office had a thick stench of cigarette smoke, and there were several butts in an ashtray on his desk. "*Hola*," he said, standing and shaking their hands. "You're American, eh? Here for the festival?"

"I'm American. Sean, here, is Irish," she said, sitting down on the vinyl chair he offered. Behind Perez, Diana noticed two pictures on his cluttered wall—one of Alfredo De Leon, the other of Luis Castrovilla. "You manage the two best matadors in Pamplona?"

He nodded and smiled proudly. "I manage all the best ones."

"My name is Diana. I just wanted to ask you a few questions about De Leon."

He tutted. "It's a shame. We're all very much in shock, here. My best matador."

Sean spotted something on the wall and let out a loud hoot. "Aha! You were at Chichén Itzá, too?"

Diana glared at him as she started to ask Perez her first question. It was no use. The man was already turning to look at the photograph of him and some others, standing in front of the ruins. "*Sí*. Me and my wife and friends. We went to Mexico last May."

Okay, now that the pleasantries were over with, she could commence with the questioning. "So—"

"I went on a cruise through the Caribbean one year and we had a trip up there. They stopped at a village afterwards and I tell you, those little villagers know their tequila. We did a tasting, and I had some that would knock your socks off. Made with ghost pepper, I—"

"Sean," Diana reminded gently. "I think Mr. Perez is probably a very busy man. And—"

"I did a tequila tasting, too!" Perez said with a smile. "I brought a cask of chocolate tequila home with us. It was good."

Diana stared, feeling like a third wheel as Sean shook his head with the memory of the other tequila. "I'm telling you, that ghost pepper stuff? That was strong. I was out of my mind for the rest of the day. Could've danced naked on the poop deck, for all I know."

They were both grinning and laughing. Diana watched them, now, waiting for them to finish. Finally, they all turned and looked at her as if she was a stranger who'd just appeared. Sean said, "Sorry, Love. You can continue."

She sighed, hating to be the Debbie Downer, raining on their parade. "Thanks. So Alfredo Leon was a good matador?"

"Very good. One of the best, not just in my eyes, but in everyone's. The mass being said for him at the bullring today is well deserved, as he had many admirers. I could always count on him to give a good show, you know?" He exhaled slowly. "I can't tell you how bad the canceling of the fights is for my business. If the bullfighters don't fight, they don't get paid. If they don't get paid, *I* don't get paid. This couldn't have happened at a worse time."

*You're really broken up about him,* Diana thought a little sourly. "So you weren't really close?"

"Were we friends? Is that what you are asking?" He laughed and leaned back far in his chair. "No. I had a friendship with many of my clients. I'm godfather to several of their children. Luis Castrovilla is one of my favorite people. But De Leon didn't have friends. He saw himself as too important. I managed his business. That was all."

"That doesn't sound good," Diana said.

He shrugged. "The man was arrogant. He knew it. He didn't care if people liked him. And so what I felt about him was irrelevant."

"So he probably had enemies?" Sean put in.

"More than most people, I am sure," the man said. "He was a matador. Every fight, every matador has dozens of those animal rights activists, following them out, spitting on them and calling them names. He'd been a bullfighter for years, though. He grew a tough skin. Never bothered him, as far as I knew."

"So other than the activists . . ." Diana said, leaning forward.

"A few other people. The other bullfighters were competition, of course, so some of them might have been jealous. And women. He had a lot of women who were jealous when he married his lovely new wife, Carolina, earlier this year," the manager said.

"Yes, but it's likely none of those people would have murdered him with an enormous bull," Diana said, repeating Carolina's words. "Where were you when you heard about what happened?"

"Same as everyone else. I was on the course, closer to the ring, waiting for the first fights to start. We were wondering where De Leon was, because he was late. And then we heard the rumors . . . which unfortunately turned out to be true." He sighed. "That's why you can rule out most of the matadors. I told the police that, too. They were all at the ring, preparing for the event. Which was where De Leon was supposed to be. I can't imagine what was going through his mind. Why he was there. It makes no sense."

That bit of information did rule out quite a few people. "Can you think of anyone else who would have done it?"

He shook his head, thinking. "The police asked me all this, too. And I tell you what I told them. This was an unfortunate accident. Someone opened the wrong barrier and the animal slipped through. That's all there is to it."

Diana shook her head. "I think whoever did it might've hoped that was the case, but the fact is, *El Gordo* was not supposed to be out there on the course. Someone jimmied the lock and let the bull out, then shuttled it to the part of the course it wasn't supposed to be."

Perez's eyes narrowed. "So that's why the police keep poking around. I wondered."

"What about his wife?" Sean put in. "You think she might have done something like this, for the insurance money?"

Perez laughed. "What insurance? No matador is insurable. Their lives are too dangerous. Believe me, Alfredo De Leon was worth much more to her alive, than dead."

"Well, maybe she had a lover . . ." Sean said, a little less surely this time. He was *really* pushing the Carolina De Leon-as-murderer theory.

"Now, that's true," Perez said with a nod. "She was a lovely woman and probably had many male admirers. But the times I saw them together, I truly believed they were in love."

That was news to Diana. Maybe she'd have to see them together, but Carolina only seemed to love herself, and De Leon, the only time she'd met him, seemed so *angry*. She couldn't picture them as lovebirds.

"Well, thank you," Diana said, standing. "I don't want to take any more of your time."

He nodded. "I hope you find out what happened to him. I can't believe that someone would do this on purpose . . . even if De Leon wasn't the nicest man on Earth, I'm sorry he's dead."

*You're sorry you won't be collecting a paycheck from him,* Diana thought as she bid him goodbye, and Sean opened the door for her to step outside. She waved to the receptionist and looked at Sean.

Sean winced. "I don't like that look in your eyes," he said with a sly smile. "I think it means there's trouble brewing. Where do you want to go next?"

"Not far. And hopefully, there won't be any trouble. But I think it's time we talk to some of those activists."

# CHAPTER THIRTEEN

By the time they left Juan Perez's office, it was already mid-afternoon. The crowds outside had increased, and despite the absence of bullfights, people were streaming into the arena. Diana checked her watch and realized it was almost time for the De Leon memorial to begin. "Do you think we should go in?" she asked. "Just for a few minutes?"

Sean shrugged.

They were just near the entrance when Diana spotted the humorless Detective Carrera, standing at the front entrance, monitoring everyone as they walked inside. No doubt, he'd want to talk to her.

She turned away. "You know what? On second thought, let's see if we can find the activists."

The activists were now standing away from the entrance gates to the arena, behind barriers set out by police. There were more standing outside than when they'd entered Perez's office, and they were chanting slogans in Spanish. Diana tried to speak with them, but they didn't speak English, and seemed annoyed by her presence. Though Sean could speak Spanish, she wasn't sure he was asking the right questions. Besides, she wasn't sure the activists were taking him seriously, in that hat.

Finally, she said, "I think our best bet is to find that Rachel Hawkins. But I don't see her here."

Sean nodded and said to one of the activists, *"Dónde está Rachel Hawkins?"*

The man spoke quickly and pointed wildly in different directions.

Sean listened, frowning. "He said she went off to her hotel and she's not expected back here."

"Okay. Where's her hotel?"

"That's the problem. He doesn't know. He says he thinks it's somewhere along the festival route, but he's not sure. Somewhere close by."

Diana looked around and let out a long sigh. "That's not really helpful! The festival is huge. There are blocks and blocks of hotels she could've gone back to."

Sean nodded. "A bit like looking for a needle in a stack of needles, I'd say. What if we—"

"How about if we split up?" she asked suddenly. She knew what he was going to suggest—relaxing with another beer. And if she did that, she'd probably never get up again. She was already getting tired from her early afternoon beer, and she needed to get answers. Plus, it wasn't like Sean was getting on her nerves—well, not that much—but she had a feeling he was just putzing around, wanting to relax. And she was far too Type A for that. She could make a lot more headway, striking out on her own.

He raised an eyebrow. "You think we should?"

She nodded and pointed down a street. "I'll go that way. You go that way. Just text me if you get a hit for Rachel Hawkins. Okay?"

He pressed his lips together. "Love . . . are you unhappy with me?"

"Oh. No," she said, shaking her head.

"Are you sure. Because—"

"No. No. Of course not," she said emphatically.

He gazed at her doubtfully, took her hand, and then kissed her knuckles. "I will see you soon, then."

"Thanks," she said, and even before he'd turned around, she felt guilty.

No, he didn't seem at all invested in the investigation the way she was. But he didn't need to be. He was just being Sean. Relaxed, happy-go-lucky, completely content with letting the wind take him wherever it wished. And wasn't that what she'd vowed to be, time and time again, during this trip?

Looking at herself now, so intent on getting to the bottom of this investigation, she realized she'd failed miserably. Yes, the police suspected her of the murder. But like Pablo Arroyo said, if she was innocent, eventually, the truth would come out. Maybe she needed to stop running from place to place to speak to suspects and witnesses like a chicken with its head cut off, and at least try to enjoy some of the festival.

As she walked down the alleyway, she had the distinct impression that by getting upset and short with Sean, she'd upset *him*. After all, who wanted to go on an adventure with someone as uptight as she was?

She stopped at the first hotel, but even as she entered, she knew it was the wrong place. With its golden chandeliers and lush carpeting, it seemed a little too fancy and upscale for the laid-back hippie woman like Rachel Hawkins. She already knew what would happen when she approached and asked at the front desk. Sure enough, there was no one by that name staying there.

After the third hotel, she'd begun to get a little discouraged. Rachel Hawkins wasn't like her. She likely wasn't the type to have to reserve a place months ahead of time for fear of one's only available accommodations be a park bench. In fact, someone like Rachel Hawkins probably *preferred* park benches. Who knew . . . maybe she was sleeping in some tent city on the outskirts of Pamplona's border. In that case, maybe they'd never find her.

Scanning the area, she wondered where the nearest hostel was. That seemed more like Rachel Hawkins's style.

Just as she approached the next hotel, which already looked like another no-go, from the fancy script sign outside, her phone rang. It was Bea, her youngest. She lifted the phone to her ear. "Bea! How are you?"

"Fine, Mom. But we're wondering about you. We've all been talking, and no one has heard a peep from you since before you arrived in Barcelona. Is everything all right?"

"Oh, yes. Everything's just great," she said, deciding to skip that hotel and go on to the next one. "You all worry about me too much."

"I know, I know! But you're our mom! So we worry about you. And how many times did you call me when I first arrived in Japan? Believe me, I was sick of you, too."

Diana's heart palpitated at the memory of seeing her youngest off at JFK to begin her new life, teaching in Japan. "But you were so young. Only twenty-two, heading out to live in a new country by yourself?"

"This isn't much different," Bea pointed out. "There are plenty of people who'd like to take advantage of a lone, middle-aged tourist."

"Oh, you sound like Lily. She thought for sure I was going to meet a serial killer, or white slavers, of—"

90

"Lily's just ridiculous. But it's true. If you don't call us regularly, how do we know that you're okay and not lying dead in a ditch somewhere?"

Diana smiled. At least they all hadn't decided to fly out to Spain to be there with her. That's what had happened in Italy. "I'm fine. Don't worry. Just very busy with all the, uh . . . sightseeing."

"Are you having fun in Barcelona?"

"Oh. I'm not there. I'm in Pamplona. For the festival of St. Fermin."

"You mean the Running of the Bulls? That doesn't sound up your alley at all. How did you wind up there?"

"Well, it's a funny story. I met an Irish gentleman who—"

"Mom! You met a man?"

"Yes, I did. A very nice one. And he invited me to come here for the festival. So that's where I've been. And—"

"Mom. You vixen! Who is he? Are you falling in love?"

She laughed. Lily would've told her mother that she needed to run away, that he could be a serial killer, but Bea was a romantic. "No, Darling. It's not that. He's just a friend," she said, quickly changing the subject. "How is the wedding planning going?"

Bea grumbled. "Ugh. I hate it. I hate planning events like this. I wish I was back with you, solving murders, like we did in Italy. That was so much fun."

"It was, wasn't it?"

"I think it was the highlight of my life. Really."

Diana smiled. She'd never had as much fun solving a murder she was accused of than when she was with Bea, rushing all over Verona, intent on finding the murderer. Bea was as high-energy and Type A as she was. It was on the tip of her tongue to tell her about this newest murder, but she knew Bea would probably try to come out and see her, in Spain. And with her wedding coming up, Bea had enough to worry about. "Well, I'll be sure to text you and let you know where I am, more often. Okay?"

"Okay. Bye, Mommy. Have fun. Don't cross any of those bulls."

As she ended the call, Diana thought, *Too late.*

Then she realized she had a message from Sean. She looked at it, half-expecting to hear that he'd given up on the search and was now relaxing under an umbrella somewhere, with a cold cerveza.

Instead, she saw this message: *Bingo. Meet me at 1201 C. de los Teobaldos.*

Her jaw dropped. So he'd found Rachel Hawkins? And here, she thought she'd find him, later on, nursing another beer at some outdoor café, and enjoying the festival.

She plugged the address into her GPS, and broke into a run, following its directions.

Ten minutes later, she arrived at a run-down area of the city, where there was an old brick-façade building with a faded sign that said, *Jesus y Maria Hostal.*

She knew it. A hostel. This would definitely be more up Rachel Hawkins' alley. The windows were covered by a dirty shade, but as she stepped inside, she saw Sean, deep in conversation with the female clerk. She giggled, clearly charmed.

He turned to her. "*Macushla!*" he shouted across the sparsely decorated lobby.

Scanning the area for Rachel Hawkins, Diana nearly stepped on several people sitting on the floor of the place as she made her way to Sean. There were people all over the place, carrying bags, unshaven, clothing unkempt, and the place smelled a little like body odor. It looked a bit like a refugee camp. But no Rachel.

"Hi, did you find anything?" she asked, gritting her teeth.

It only occurred to her when he made a face that she was doing it again. Being her normal, uptight, Type A personality. He said, "Relax and cool yourself down a bit, Lass, and I'll explain everything."

"Sorry," Diana said with a sigh. "I really just want to figure out who did this. It stinks to be a suspect. I keep worrying they'll track me down and arrest me in the middle of the night, and by then there'll be nothing I can do to prove my innocence."

"I understand," he said, taking her hand and patting it.

"So . . . Rachel? You said you found her?"

He shook his head. "She's not here."

Diana's spirits sank, and then confusion seeped in. She held up her phone. "But if she isn't here, then why did you write me that—"

"She's not here now. But she *was* here, earlier," Sean said, pointing to the woman who was standing behind the messy clerk's desk, smiling at them. "Juanita, here, does not speak English.  But from what I gather, Rachel Hawkins stayed here for three nights. She got here before the festival began."

"Where did she go? Is she coming back?"

"Turns out, she wasn't very happy. She made a big stink about the whole festival and created a lot of commotion. Poor Juanita even had to call the police here, once, because Rachel Hawkins wouldn't shut up about how everyone participating in the festival had blood on their hands. She was screaming at anyone and everyone who she could about how barbaric the event was," Sean said with a shrug. "And eventually, this morning, she decided she'd had enough. She couldn't stay in Pamplona for another minute. She packed up her things and left."

"She just left?" Diana's eyes widened. "That sounds a little suspicious, doesn't it?"

"More than a little," Sean agreed.

"Just great. We have to find her. Do you have any idea where she went?" she asked the clerk, forgetting that she couldn't speak English.

The clerk simply smiled and nodded.

Sean said, "Diana, Love. I asked that. And she *did* say where she was going. But I'm afraid it's not going to be easy to track her down."

"Why not? Oh, don't tell me she went back to America?"

"No. She's still in the country. But Rachel Hawkins is a nomad. She doesn't stay in one place for very long. And she said she was going on The Way."

"The way where?"

"The Way," Sean said, a little more forcefully. "The Way of St. James. The Camino de Santiago."

Diana shook her head. "I'm sorry. What is that?"

"It's a pilgrimage route to Santiago de Compostela, on the Northern coast of Spain. Thousands of people make the trek through Europe every year. It's supposed to be a life-changing trip of reflection and spiritual awakening."

"Santiago . . . You mean the Cathedral you were mentioning, before, with that incense burner?"

"Yes, that's right. It's—"

"So why couldn't we just follow her—"

"It's very hard. There isn't just one route. There are many. And so many different stops along the way that one might make, it would be very difficult to find her," he explained. "Even so, Juanita here said she was cleaning her room and found this."

He handed her a crumpled brochure which said, *El Camino de Santiago*. Someone had written in the margins of it and had circled a couple of the hotels and various points of interest along the way. "We can check these out, right? How far away are they?"

"They're not in Pamplona, that's for sure," Sean said. "And didn't you say that the police told you not to leave the area because you might be needed for questioning?"

She nodded. "Yes, but . . ."

"I could go for you," Sean suggested. "If you really think it's that important. I could take the trail and ask a few people as I—"

"No!" she said. She had a feeling if she did that, she'd never see him again. Or he'd find a great place to drink, forget what his purpose was and disappear on the trail, never to be found again. "I think I can go."

Sean grinned. "There's my good chancer. You're going to go out on the lam, huh?"

"Shh!" she said, looking around, not that there was anyone nearby to hear them. "But yes. I mean, it's very suspicious that that woman would just leave like that. She had a reason to want him dead, too, and she obviously has a bit of a temper. I think it's the best lead we have. And the police are too busy dealing with all the other traffic from the festival. I think it's our duty to check it out."

He let out a long, raucous laugh. "All right, Love. If you say so, then let's do it!"

She shook her head. "No. I think I should probably do it on my own."

He tilted his head. "On your own? Are you looking for a religious experience, too?"

She wasn't sure. Maybe because this was the Way of St. James, but she felt for sure it was the answer to what had happened to De Leon. And maybe, if she was lucky, it'd provide her with her own spiritual awakening, too, making her feel as though she'd found everything she came to Europe to achieve. That would be nice.

Whatever it was, she felt like she had to do it on her own.

"You can go back to the hotel, in case the police show up, and if they ask about me, you can tell them I'm around Pamplona somewhere, and will be back shortly. If they can't find either of us for a long time, they could get suspicious. In fact, I'm worried they're already suspicious since we haven't been at the hotel since earlier this morning."

"Likely, but you don't know that trail. It can be rather—"

"I'll be fine. If you just point me in the direction of it, I'll find my way."

"If you say so," he said, but she couldn't mistake the doubt in his voice.

They went outside, and he pointed her up the street. "Up that way is where the Pilgrim's Way passes through Pamplona. It crosses the Arga River at the La Magdalena Gothic Bridge and passes the 1553 French Gate and Bastion del Redin. It then weaves its way in front of the Baroque façade of Pamplona's City Hall, a favorite stopping-off point in the center of town, and the Church of San Cernin of Toulouse." He handed her a map. "It's all in here. You just keep following it. You'll probably see other pilgrims on the trek. Look for the shell symbol if you get off-course."

She nodded. It sounded easy. "Sure. I can do that."

He shook her hand. "Good luck, *macushla*. May the wind be at your back, and may God be with you."

"Thanks. I probably won't be long," she said. *Though who knows? What if I'm so captivated by this trek that I can't stop going . . .* "I don't want you getting in any trouble with the local police over me not being there!"

"Good thinking," he said, holding up his phone. "I'll text you if I see them."

She nodded and turned away from him, starting up the street, and as she did, she shivered a little despite the late day heat. She'd never been one to take chances and yet she'd found taking them, over the past couple months, to be exhilarating. But this was outright breaking the law. Could she do it?

She walked toward the city limits, unsure. But she was about to find out.

# CHAPTER FOURTEEN

Somehow, when she set foot on The Way of St. James, Diana thought that her life would change. She thought that a glowing light would come down from the heavens and show her that she was on the right path.

But it turned out, a bit disappointingly, that the Way wasn't all that life-affirming or soul-changing.

In fact, it was just like any other walk she'd taken while in Europe. *Well, what did you expect, Diana? You've only gone like, half a mile. You haven't even left Pamplona yet. I bet if you followed this to the end of the line, you'd find exactly what you're looking for.*

She also felt like she was getting another blister, despite the comfortable shoes that she'd been given by Evan's fiancé, Tilda, in Verona.

But the views were beautiful. Once she left the city proper and left the hubbub of the city and the festival behind her, the landscape grew greener and lusher, with plenty of shade trees and flowers in bloom. The city sights gave way to small-town charm, with quaint storefronts and squares with stone benches and fountains. There were gothic stone churches, moss-covered stone walls, old barns, and tiny houses with thatched roofs, nestled along the banks of the Arga River. She took a deep breath, inhaling the scent of grass and fresh air instead of the festival smells, and smiled.

Yes, this was the Way of St. James. It had her name written all over it. If that wasn't a sign, what was? She was sure that it was like the pot of gold at the end of the rainbow . . . the arrow pointing her to where she needed to be.

But though the sights were welcome, the one sight she desperately wanted to see—Rachel Hawkins—eluded her. Rachel stood out, with her long, curly hair and bright, loose skirts. But she didn't pass a single person that even resembled the woman.

Unfolding the map, she carefully followed it, but it wasn't hard. There was another couple, about fifty yards ahead, that seemed to be going the same way. They were younger and she had to quicken her pace to keep up with them, so by the time she reached the bridge Sean had spoken of, she was out of breath.

*Forget it. I'm going to drop dead if I keep trying to follow those people,* she said, slumping alongside the bridge and fanning her face.

She reached into her bag, thankful that she'd kept a bottle of water with her, from the previous day. It was warm, but welcome. She sipped it slowly, deciding it was best to save it, since she didn't know how long this trek would take her.

Spying the mountains around the town, she wondered if this route would take her into them. If so, she was woefully underprepared.

Oh. Maybe that was what Sean was talking about when he'd said that she didn't know the trail. She didn't, really. If she was going to take this route, for real, she'd need to have a real backpack, like the rest of the travelers. Hiking shoes. An idea of where to stop and what to see. A better itinerary. This wasn't some path a person took on a whim.

Opening up the brochure, she tried to read what was written on it. *More than 300,000 people a year travel The Way of St. James on a life-changing trek though the Spanish countryside. Choose your way—it is a journey made in the spirit of adventure, enlightenment, friendship, and shared experience!*

She flipped through the pages. So it turned out, there was more than one Way, but they all led to the same place. And from what she could see, she was on the French Way. But there were many different routes and outposts one could take on each journey.

So, in essence, it was probably going to be very difficult to find Rachel Hawkins. If she'd left earlier that day, she likely had several hours head-start, and who knew where a free spirit like her would choose to stop off.

*This is probably a waste of my time,* she thought, taking a big gulp of water, this time and looking around. Even though it might have been a waste, something about the place pulled at her. She ached to continue the journey.

The narrow, arched bridge was a picture—she was sure she'd seen it on a calendar somewhere. It was only a footbridge, covered in black moss, spanning the still green river. It looked like something out of a fairy tale. Swatting away a fly, Diana leaned there, waiting for her breathing to return to normal.

As she did, she saw a woman, standing on the stone bridge. She had her arms out, like she was getting ready to jump.

Diana straightened, heart thumping. Was she . . . it couldn't be, but that looked like . . . a suicide in progress?

As she moved closer, away from the shade of the trees, she noticed the abundant mass of curly, graying hair, tied up in a loose headwrap, the long flowing skirt . . . was that Rachel Hawkins?

Of course. Now it all made sense. She'd killed that matador and couldn't live with herself because of the guilt. She'd come out here to end it all.

And Diana was about to be a witness to it.

Her first instinct was to scream the woman's name, but she bit her tongue. She didn't want to startle her. One wrong move, and who knew what she'd do?

So she inched closer, ever-so-slowly, looking both ways to see if anyone was coming over the bridge. But they were alone.

When she got to the base of the bridge, she said, softly. "Please. Don't do it."

The woman didn't look back. She didn't move a muscle. It was almost as if she hadn't heard Diana at all.

Diana took another step forward, and spoke, louder: "Please. It's not worth it."

Again, no answer.

As she got closer, she realized that the green river wasn't even that far down. Twenty feet, at most. The woman might break something, but as far as killing herself? That'd probably be a stretch.

Again, Diana looked up and down the path for someone else to help her. But there was no one. So, once she got close enough, she took a deep breath and made a decision.

The woman's skirt blew in the breeze, and she seemed to waver there, like a top, before she fell over.

Before she could, Diana sprang forward, bear-hugging the woman's knees.

"What?" the woman shrieked suddenly as Diana pulled her back with all her might. The two went crashing to the stone bottom of the footbridge.

Safe and sound.

But before Diana could let out that breath she'd been holding in relief, the woman started to pummel her in the shoulder with both of her fists. "What are you, crazy!" she shouted at Diana, scowling. "What were you doing?"

"I was saving you," Diana returned in shock. "Of all the places to commit suicide—"

"Suicide! I wasn't going to jump, you idiot! I'd barely get a bruise if I jumped from that bridge! I was meditating!" she groused. "The breeze is beautiful up there!" She yanked her skirt away, which happened to be caught under Diana's knee. "Great. You ripped my skirt."

Diana jumped to her feet. "Oh. I'm—I'm sorry."

"You should be." She reached down and grabbed her worn canvas messenger bag, throwing it over her shoulder and harrumphing in indignation.

Peals of laughter rose up around them. Suddenly, there was a small crowd of pilgrims around them, watching the sight of the two middle-aged women, wrestling on the path. Diana's heart was pounding out a mad drumbeat, so she clasped a hand over it as she watched the woman break through the crowd and continue on her way.

Forcing off the embarrassment, Diana broke into a jog and met up with her. "Really, I'm sorry. Let me pay for your skirt."

The woman rolled her eyes and said in disgust. "Americans are all the same. Think they can make things better with money." She shook her head. "Money is of no interest to me. It's people. Nature. Being at one with Mother Earth. Which I was *trying* to do back there, before I was so rudely interrupted."

"Oh. I didn't realize."

"Of course you didn't." She stopped and gave Diana the once-over. "You're a typical American. Self-absorbed, only interested in the trappings of wealth. There's a higher purpose in this world, and I only hope you'll find it."

She turned and continued to march along. As she did, she swept a hand down and picked a blade of grass.

"Is that why you're travelling The Way?" Diana asked, catching up with her.

She shrugged as she wove the grass into a braid. "It's not religious for me, since I'm a humanist. But it's not about religion for a lot of people. It's about discovering one's place in the world. Who one is. 'That the powerful play goes on, and you might contribute a verse,' in the words of Walt Whitman." She smiled thoughtfully. "Too many people plod through life without recognizing their purpose. They don't contribute, not because they can't but because they don't pay attention to what it is they're here for. And that's sad, don't you think?"

She nodded. "Yes, it is."

"Nature is telling you. The Earth is screaming it to you. But few people take the time to actually listen." She hooked a thumb behind her. "That was what I was doing back there."

"Oh," Diana said, feeling foolish for interrupting her. "Did you learn anything?"

"Nothing that I haven't already known. My verse is to speak out for those who don't have voices. That's what I was doing in Pamplona, at the bullring." She eyed Diana suspiciously. "What are you doing here? Have you been following me?"

Diana was tired. At first, Rachel had seemed like a good prospect, but now, all she saw in front of her was a gentle person who loved life and wouldn't harm any living creature. She explained, awkwardly, "Well, the police think that I might have had something to do with Alfredo De Leon's death. And I saw how disgusted you'd been by him, and when I heard you left abruptly, I wondered if—"

"You thought *I* killed him?" She laughed bitterly. "Oh, my, honey. No, that's barking up the wrong tree, I'll tell you. In fact, I heard a matador was killed, but didn't realize it was that one outside the bullring. Was it really him?"

She nodded.

"Oh. That's a shame. I mean, of all the ways to be taught a lesson. I don't like to see anyone suffer, but I suppose if you mess with the bull . . ."

"You get the horns," Diana finished.

Rachel nodded. "It wasn't me, though. The police interviewed me and cleared me. I was with a couple of friends at the Oteiza Museum."

"The Ot—"

"Oteiza Museum. It's outside of Pamplona. He was a wonderful artist," she said with a smile. "After we did our little protest, we

100

decided to get away from it all so we wouldn't have to see the bloodshed, so we took a bus there. We all had our tickets stamped. So it couldn't have been any of us."

"Oh. I see."

"I'm sorry if you got the wrong idea. I left so quickly today because I'd had enough of it. All those people, running around, celebrating the barbarism of the event. It's disgusting, if you ask me. It took its toll on me. I felt like I was suffocating and needed to get out."

"Which was why you were . . ." she pointed to the bridge.

"Right. Catching my breath. Restoring my center."

Now Diana felt even more foolish. That made sense. How often had she run off in a thousand different directions, failing to take her time and think things through? That was probably the reason why she hadn't discovered her true purpose in life. Oh, she'd done things she was proud of—had a good career, lovely children, a comfortable nest egg— but were any of those her true, actual purpose? Her verse to contribute to the world?

She looked down the trail as far as she could see, where it bent and headed up a grassy hill. "How far are you planning to go?"

Rachel grinned. "All the way. Take care!"

She practically skipped off, up the hill, leaving Diana standing there in the late-day sunshine, watching her. People may have thought she was crazy, but Rachel Hawkins didn't care. She was a woman who knew her purpose, who *lived* her purpose. For a moment, Diana longed to go with her, to follow the path of her namesake to the very end.

Then she turned back toward Pamplona. She had to get back.

She took a few steps toward the city. *This was a waste.*

But was it? Maybe not. Rachel's words about pilgrimages and finding one's purpose hung heavy in her mind. Perhaps that was why she'd been led out on this journey to begin with. Not to find her long-lost love, Stephane, but to find and fall in love with her purpose.

She spun around and scanned the trail. Rachel was already gone.

Maybe she was supposed to be here. Maybe everything had been leading her to this place.

The urge to follow the trail was almost overwhelming. She had to physically pull herself back to the city. As she did, she made a vow to herself.

One day, when she was no longer a suspect, she would come back.

It was the Way of St. James, after all. She couldn't wait to find her destiny.

*But first, I need to find out who killed De Leon.* She broke into a run, headed back to the hotel.

# CHAPTER FIFTEEN

The sun had almost set by the time Diana reached her street in the center of Pamplona. She'd past many pilgrims on their way, and each time, she felt a wistful stabbing at her heart. It only made her more anxious to solve the murder.

As she walked, her phone buzzed. There was a missed call from a familiar number—Evan. A voicemail, too. She listened to it and sighed. It was actually from Tilda, his young fiancé. Her chirpy, high-pitched voice was just the cherry on top of her annoying day. *Hi, Diana! I was just wondering if I could go over something with you! It has to do with plans for the wedding!*

It was probably something to do with the guest list, and whether she'd be needing a plus-one. She deleted the message, massaging a burgeoning headache away from her temple. She'd call her later.

The market was dark when she arrived, though gas streetlamps outside were blazing a bright, cheerful orange. She climbed the stairs to the apartment and was surprised to see the door open. Someone was speaking, inside.

When she reached the top landing, her stomach dropped.

It was Detective Carrera, and he didn't look any happier than he had the first time she met him. They were sitting at the kitchen table, surrounded by all the crates and boxes. From the way Sean was slumped there, his eyes bleary with exhaustion, it looked as if they'd been there for quite some time.

"Hello!" she said brightly, hoping to counteract his negativity. "Nice to see you, detective."

Her eyes went to Sean, who looked, for the first time, a little uneasy. His eyes seemed to transmit something telepathically to her, but she wasn't sure what. Likely, the detective was there to ask more questions about her movements the day of De Leon's death, but she didn't like the warning in Sean's eyes.

"What did we tell you about leaving town?" he barked.

She blinked. "I didn't leave town." Well, not technically. She'd skirted the edge of it, but she'd been within the city limits. "I was only at a café."

"A café? We've been looking for you, all day."

"Oh, well . . ." She looked at Sean. "I'm sure Sean told you that we did a little sightseeing. We've been around, though. We're not attempting to impede your investigation in any way."

His lips twisted. "What was this I hear about you two visiting the bullring?"

She gritted her teeth. "We just wanted a tour."

"If I didn't know better, I'd think you were trying to meddle in this investigation."

She crossed her arms. "That's not true. Right, Sean?"

Sean cleared his throat. "That's what I've been trying to tell him for the past hour. He doesn't want to listen."

Detective Carrera swung his scowl over to Sean, then pulled out his notepad, and kicked out the only open chair at the table. "Please, sit, Señora St. James. I'd like to go over your whereabouts during the crime, once again, if you wouldn't mind."

Diana was exhausted. All the walking she'd done over the past few hours had taken its toll, the day had stretched on forever, and now she wanted nothing more than to snuggle into bed. She yawned, then remembered her *bed* for the night would be with the Snoring Wonder. She'd likely have the same trouble falling asleep that she'd had the night before.

She stepped into the kitchen and sat down in the chair. "Of course. What can I tell you?"

"I would just like to fill in some holes that I have in the timeline. After you saw De Leon in front of the bullring and he accosted you, where did you go?"

She looked over at Sean. "To the start of the race. It was almost time."

"Alone?"

"No. Sean was with me."

Carrera looked over at Sean. Sean nodded. "It says here that you ran with the bulls."

She nodded.

"*You*, ran with the bulls?" He repeated. This time, there was an incredulous tone to his words.

"Yes, I did."

"Pardon my saying so, but we don't get many women running with the bulls. Particularly women of your age."

Diana stared at him, in shock. "What, are you saying that women shouldn't—"

"I'm saying its dangerous, especially considering—"

Sean said, "Well, she did it. And she faced up those bulls right better than I did. I got conked on the head and missed most of the fun."

Diana smiled at him, grateful, but then glared at the detective. "I can do anything I'd like to do, whether it be run with a bunch of bulls, scale a mountain, or even take a pilgrimage alone into a country I've never been to before. I'm not some helpless damsel in distress, who needs to be told what to do. That's not how I'll find my purpose, following people around all my life."

Her voice had been steadily rising, something she only realized when she pounded the table with her fist, and it shook.

They just stared at her.

She tucked a lock of wayward hair demurely behind her ear. "I just don't like the insinuation that I can't do certain things because I'm a woman, and because of my age."

"I'm not insinuating that you can't do these things. In fact, I see it very plausible that you could've murdered Alfredo De Leon."

She bit her tongue. She'd walked right into that one. "And how do you see that?"

"Because you were at the starting line when the first gun went off."

Diana waited for more. It didn't come. Then she said, "So? I don't see what difference it makes in the investigation if I was there, or not?"

"I'll tell you what difference it makes," the detective said, pocketing his notebook. "The lock of the *El Gordo's* pen was pried open without the key. After that was done, there was likely only one place for whoever opened the gate to go without being noticed. And that was with everyone else, to the front of the race."

Diana's eyes widened. "That's ridiculous. There were so many people, and so much chaos, and--"

"And yet you were both near the corral when the lock was tampered with, *and* in the same location off the course where the body was found. Very strange, yes?"

Now, she understood. Yes, that was a remarkable coincidence. "Just bad luck," she muttered.

Sean said, "I'm sure there were cameras all over the place during the run, though? Have you gone through the footage?"

Detective Carrera looked at the Irishman like he was an idiot. "Of course. We've spent the past day combing through all of the evidence, which includes hours and hours of footage. Unfortunately, we find nothing of the beginning of the race, or the area of the barrier that was removed. And we see nothing of *you*."

His gaze narrowed on Diana.

Of course. Somehow, the camera seemed to have an aversion to her. She picked up the newspaper and showed it to him. "I was right next to this guy, without the pants. That's my elbow. I think."

The detective looked at it without much interest. "Unfortunately, we cannot make a positive identification based on an elbow."

That was pretty much what she thought he'd say.

"And I've done a little searching on you, Señora St. James," he said, to which Diana winced. "It seems that you had similar troubles in Paris? And in Verona?"

Sean's eyes widened. She looked at the ground. "Don't forget Austria," she offered. What was the difference? He knew everything, already. "But in all of those incidents, the murderer was found. And it wasn't me."

"You *do* have bad luck, don't you?" Sean put in.

*You have no idea,* she thought, letting out a sigh. *Maybe this is what comes from not living my true purpose.*

He stood up to leave. "I'll be making a few more inquiries. But I must stress, and can't stress enough" he said, holding a finger in her face. "That you need to stay put. We will have more questions for you, I am sure."

"Right. I will," she mumbled, feeling beaten. "Are you saying that you don't have any other suspects?"

He pressed his lips together, and for a moment she thought he wouldn't answer. Then he said, "We have several leads that we are following. That's all I am at liberty to say."

*Several leads,* she thought. *And I'll bet I am the most promising one of all of them.*

# CHAPTER SIXTEEN

After the detective left, Diana wandered into the kitchen to find Sean, dotting his ruddy forehead with a napkin. He was sweating, taking deep breaths, as if he'd just been in a near-miss accident.

"Is everything okay?" she asked.

He nodded. "It's just . . ." He fanned his face. "Bugger. I'm not used to lying to the police like that. I thought that detective was onto me."

She blinked, surprised. Here, he'd been so happy-go-lucky, so cavalier about all of the calamities that had plagued them. The idea of getting a horn up his fanny had thrilled him. Nothing caused a ripple or made him worry in the least. And yet here he was, afraid of a police detective?

*Maybe my problem is that I've been grilled by too many police detectives before. I'm starting to get used to it.*

Seeing him worrying like this made her wonder if she was worrying enough. She'd been lucky so far. But what if this was the time her luck ran out? "What did you say to them?"

"I said you stepped out, and I didn't know when you would return, but that you were around here, somewhere." He patted his chest. "I tried to be vague so I wasn't lying, but since I knew that you were on that route out of the city . . ."

"Well, that's not a lie. I didn't even leave the city. Well, not really. I came close to the border, but I don't actually think I crossed it. So all's good. Calm down." She never thought she'd be the one, saying those words to him.

"All right. So I gather you didn't find the activist woman?"

"Oh, no. I did. But it didn't do much good."

"No?"

She told him the whole story about how she'd met Rachel Hawkins on the bridge and thought she was in the midst of a suicide attempt. It was embarrassing, but she knew it would cheer Sean up, and was right.

He laughed and slapped his knee when she finished. "Yeah, so she was just meditating. I'm an idiot."

"That's a good one."

"Anyway, so she wasn't around during the running of the bulls. She was at a museum. And the reason she left was because she got fed up with the barbarism and just needed to get out," Diana explained with a sigh. "So let me ask you. You mentioned the pilgrimage of St. James before. Do you know anything about it? She wasn't religious, but said she was going on it because it helped her get in tune with her purpose."

Sean nodded. "Well, I'm a Catholic myself. And I know of people who made the trip and said that it changed their spiritual lives. But lately I've been hearing about non-believers going and experiencing some kind of awakening. I don't know about that. Sounds like a lot of superstition to me."

"You think? Because I thought it sounded rather—"

"I don't believe any of that. Having to hike a trail in order to discover oneself? I think I'd have more of an awakening, sitting on the porcelain throne."

Diana frowned. "That's disgusting."

He shrugged. "I'm just speaking the truth. You don't need nice scenery in order to learn something about yourself. You just need to do something most people don't seem to want to bother with—*think*." He tapped the side of his head. "Most people are too busy for that."

She glared at him. "Then what have you been traveling around Europe for?"

"It's not for self-discovery. It's to enjoy myself. That's all. I know who I am. And that's why I went traveling alone—because I actually like my own company. There are too many people out there who can't stand to be with themselves. And why? Because they haven't been alone with themselves enough to know who they really are."

She stared at him. That was true. She'd spent all of her life, surrounded by others. It was only when she was alone that she realized she had a giant hole in her life, and it was because she really didn't know herself. She'd been afraid to go on this trip, by herself, simply because she didn't trust that she could enjoy herself on her own.

But Sean was different. He enjoyed being on his own. Thrived upon it. Didn't need anyone or any pilgrimage to tell him anything about himself. He probably didn't even need *her*, here, either, messing up his enjoyment of the festival by becoming a suspect in this murder. "Are you saying you didn't want me to come along with you?"

"Not at all. You know I wanted you to come with me. But as for going on a pilgrimage, alone, hoping to find something . . . I get the feeling most people who walk those steps wind up disappointed."

Diana hugged herself. That's what this entire trip to Europe had been, after all. A pilgrimage. And yes, so far, she hadn't found very much. . . except trouble. She'd found a lot of trouble. She'd seen a lot of places and learned she could survive on her own.

But as she'd walked even that small part of The Way, she'd had the feeling that maybe she was missing out. Maybe the idea of it wasn't to just float around Europe and pick up whatever she fancied. Maybe what she needed to do is take an actual, tried-and-true route.

"How do you know that's true, if you've never done it?"

He smiled at her. "I know a thing or two, Lass."

"The people that I saw on it seemed, I don't know, at peace. Excited. You sound very cynical about it. I never thought of you as a cynic."

He yawned and stretched his arms over his head. "I'm all for people exploring, broadening their horizons. But I don't know that it'll suddenly make someone a better person. It takes more than one's scenery to do that." He shrugged. "I suppose I'm getting so cynical only because I'm knackered. I tell you, I'm going to be dead to the world tonight."

*Oh, no.* Her ex, Evan, always snored loudest when he was *really* tired. "You know what I think," she said, looking around. "I think I will clear out these boxes and sleep on the couch."

He stared at her. "Are you angry at me?"

"No," she said with a shrug, shoving a box of canned potatoes to the ground to expose an awfully ugly, lumpy loveseat of matted orange velour. "I just think I'd get a better night's sleep out here."

He leaned against the door jamb and watched her. "You're angry. Because I spoke my mind about the pilgrimage, is that it? I called it nonsense and rubbish and you don't see it that way. It's something you really wanted to do?"

"No," she insisted, tugging on another crate. Though she was *going* to be, if he didn't help her get the couch clear. These crates weighed a ton. "I don't know what I want to do. I don't even know if I want to be here."

"Ah. That's it. You're fed up with ol' Sean, ready to give him the ol' heave ho. Admit it."

She finally succeeded in getting the next crate on the ground, narrowly missing crushing her toe. She looked up and sighed. "I'm not! I'm just really tired, too. Can we table any more discussion until—"

"I don't think so."

She looked up. "What?"

"Well, I was raised in a household where you don't go to bed angry. And you're angry. This is our first fight. We need to talk it out and come to a resolution before bed. And that's final."

She blinked. Since when did sharing a flat as roommates constitute a household? And their first fight? Meaning there would be more? That made them almost sound like . . . a couple?

Immediately, she softened. She said, "It's not a fight. I promise. And I am not angry at you. I think I'm more angry at myself, for exactly what you said. Thinking that I could trek around the world and discover something new about myself I couldn't have discovered back home in New York. It doesn't work that way."

"Ah, *macushla,*" he said, coming over to her. He easily removed the last two crates from the couch and put an arm around her. Together, they sat on it, sinking into the mushy, overused cushions. He patted her knee. "I think you feel like you're broken, and this trip was going to fix something. But the fact is, you were perfectly fine, all along."

She shrugged doubtfully, unable to meet his eyes.

"What has broken you has been all these crimes happening during your vacation. It's no wonder you're out of sorts. But anyone would be. In front of me, I see a woman who is strong, courageous, and who has found herself pretty well, I'd say." He winked. "A right good chancer."

Butterflies swarmed her stomach, and she smiled. "Thank you."

"But I do think that if you're feeling that way, it's because you've been rushing around like a madwoman, trying to solve this murder. I say you should give it up. Let the police do what they need to do. You're innocent. We know that. So let them find it out."

She nodded reluctantly. She didn't want to, but she didn't see any other choice. And she was so tired. "I suppose I should. I don't really have any ideas where to go next. It's all dead ends. I can't even think of who else I'd ask or where else I could look for clues. Everything we've done, the police seem to have already thought of. So you're right."

"I am?" He seemed surprised. "Brilliant. Well, I guess even a broken clock is right once or twice a day. So we can go to bed?"

She stood up, stretching her arms over her head. Suddenly, she felt wide awake, as if she'd been jolted by an electric current. Something still swam inside her, uneasy. The thought of abandoning the investigation, as right as Sean probably was, also made her feel . . . even more lost than before.

"Actually, I'm not so tired anymore. I think I want to take a walk."

"A walk? You haven't walked enough all over Pamplona, today?"

She laughed. "I'm fine. I just need to clear my head. And I had a call from my ex's fiancé. I should probably give her a call back before she accuses me of being difficult."

"All right . . . you'll be okay?"

She tilted her head. Hadn't she just gotten done yelling at Detective Carrera for assuming she couldn't take care of herself? "Yes, I'll be fine. Why?"

"The streets of Pamplona turn into one big party during the St. Fermin festival. It can get pretty rowdy, you know. Just be careful. There has been a rash of crime out there in recent years."

Well, she couldn't fault him for that. He was just looking after her well-being. "I will. Thanks."

She went down the stairs and stepped outside, onto the street. Sure enough, the cancelation of the bull run and the fights had not put a damper on the nightlife. Now that the sun had set, young men and women were roaming the street, beers in hand, as if this were fraternity row. Loud dance music was being piped in from outdoor speakers, with a hard beat that reverberated in Diana's chest. The mood outside was electric.

She wandered away from the crowds, up the street. Why was she worrying? There was no reason to, if she was simply going to take Sean's advice. Give up, enjoy all Pamplona had to offer, and let the police handle things.

Instead, her heart squeezed at the thought. What if they handled things, and never found the killer? What if it ended up in a cold case file, and never cleared her name? Would she be stuck in Pamplona forever, waiting for answers?

As right as Sean was that all of these crimes had taken a toll on her, she didn't think it possible to just walk away. Not when there was a murderer on the loose, and she was still a suspect.

Shivering, she walked down the street, skirting crowds of drunken revelers. Someone had to have seen something. And one of them could've been a murderer.

No, though this was a trip to find herself, there was one thing about herself she didn't have to look for. She *knew* she was inquisitive. Curious. She couldn't give up until she had all the answers. That would never change.

That meant she that she needed to find answers. And she would, just as she had done before. But how?

*

Tilda answered the phone immediately. "Oh, Diana! So happy to hear your voice."

Diana had reasons to be wary about Tilda. Not only was she her ex-husband's fiancé, but she'd gone to school with Diana's youngest daughter, Bea. Though the beautiful young woman wasn't particularly intelligent, had a bit of a grating laugh, and there was the obvious question as to whether she was just after Evan for his money, Diana had come to accept the fact that saving Evan from his mistakes wasn't her business anymore. During a visit to Italy a few weeks ago, she'd come to an understanding with Tilda, and now, actually didn't mind her so much.

"Sorry . . . is it a bad time? I have no idea what time it is there, in New York!"

Tilda laughed, a sound that wasn't as grating as it once had been. Maybe it was because she was now thousands of miles away? "It's fine. It's just before dinnertime, here. Where are you, now?"

"I'm in Pamplona."

She gasped. "Oh, my gosh! How did you get down to Brazil?" Before Diana could correct her, she added, "Geez, Diana, you are such a world traveler. I am really envious of everything you've been doing. You're so brave."

Right now, Diana didn't feel very brave. "Thank you for saying so."

"Maybe you can give me tips on a great place to go for our honeymoon? We don't want to do the Caribbean again, since we were just there. And Italy's out, too, now. I want to do something *fabulous*! Something really *extra*, something we'll never forget."

"I gotcha. Something extra. I'll think about it," Diana said, knowing that Evan would spend any amount of money possible to make it happen. The man lived to spoil his new bride-to-be. "How are things going back home?"

"Oh, you know. Crazy with the wedding plans. It's actually not that easy to get twenty-seven bridesmaids in town for one weekend to go dress shopping, let alone for the wedding!"

Diana's jaw dropped. "I'm sorry, did you say twenty-seven?"

"Yep. Well, they're not all going to be bridesmaids, obviously. I loaned some of them to Evan to be grooms-women, since he didn't really have anyone to ask."

"Oh . . ."

"And I'm really having trouble finding the donkeys for a December wedding. I don't know why it's so difficult."

"Donkeys? For . . ."

"Yes, it's so fun!" She squealed. "They walk around the reception, loaded up with beer and cocktails, and people just help themselves."

Diana cringed, half-mortified for Evan, half-interested to see this spectacle, taking place. "Waiters could do that, though, and they probably wouldn't smell as bad?" she suggested.

"Now, Diana," she said with a sigh. "That would be making the event ordinary. And I want it to be something people always remember!"

Right. Well, she was definitely on her way to that. "I'm sure you'll find a way to make it very special," Diana said, looking around the dark street. The crowds were multiplying, coming closer to her. But for the first time in a long time, she was glad she wasn't in the States, having to be subjected to these kinds of woes, every day. If she had been on Long Island, she'd have had no way of escaping them. "So, you had a question for me? About the guest list?"

"Oh, not about the guest list. I wanted to ask you . . . well, my parents aren't around anymore. And I was thinking, since you've been so kind to me, kind of like a parent to me when Bea and I were growing up . . ." She paused, and in that second, Diana's stomach dropped. "Would you be interested in giving me away at the wedding?"

Diana's stomach now settled in her big toe. The girl had twenty-seven bridesmaids, and yet no one to give her away? Diana hadn't known her parents, hadn't known they'd passed away, simply because she and Bea had never been really that close. Tilda had come over to the house once or twice, for pool parties during the summer, but that was all. Truthfully, of all her school friends, Bea hadn't really liked her. "Oh, uh—wow. You don't have anyone else?"

She cringed when the words were out. It was a crude thing to say.

Tilda said, "Well, my parents were only children, and I really don't have much in the way of . . . and well, you and Evan are so close, that it just made . . ."

"Please," Diana said, feeling bad for making the girl stammer like that. She sounded so sincere. Was it possible that, without parents, Tilda looked up to her, like a mother figure? "It's an amazing honor. I'd love to. Really. So yes, I'm very happy to."

"Really?" she squealed. "Oh, that's wonderful! Thank you!"

"No, thank *you*."

"I can't wait to tell Evan. He'll be so happy. I didn't tell him I was going to ask you, but we wanted to include you in a really special way, just because you're so special to the both of us."

"I appreciate that." And to think, a few weeks ago, she'd almost been thinking of skipping the wedding entirely. "Just let me know what you need from me."

"I will!" There was a slight pause. "I was also hoping to get your input on a wedding gift for Evan. You know him best."

She did, and if she knew Evan, he'd be a bit sick over spending so much money on an event. He made a good living as a surgeon in NYC, but he never liked throwing around money like crazy. That is, until Tilda came along. "I think that the best thing you could give him would be a day out on the links, with his buddies, and a few beers at the nineteenth hole, later on."

She laughed. "You're so good! That's what he's doing for his bachelor party!" She let out a big sigh. "So what do I give him? What do you give the man who has everything?"

"He'd love something simple, that comes from your heart. That's it. You don't have to go overboard. Really. He wouldn't want that," she suggested. "He just wants your love."

"Oh, that's so nice. You see, I'd do anything for him. I want him to know that."

"If you wrote him a letter, telling him that, it would mean more to him than anything."

"Yeah," she said excitedly. "That's good. I'll do that. Would you proofread it for me?"

"Of course."

"Great! Thanks, Diana."

Diana ended the call and realized she'd gotten away from the crowds of the festival. She turned around, letting the sounds of the celebration guide her back to the apartment.

*

When she returned to the apartment, the sound of snoring shook the walls, even before she opened the front door.

When she did, Diana spotted Sean in the darkness of the living area, among the crates. His large body was draped over the tiny loveseat so that the bottom half of his legs were draped over the arm, feet dangling. He was snoring up a storm, oblivious to her.

She smiled. So he was letting her have the bedroom. What a gentleman.

She went through the kitchen and to the hall, grabbed her nightclothes, and went to the bathroom to brush her teeth. As she washed up, she looked at herself in the mirror.

*Sean is right. I'm just fine. Not broken at all. I don't need to be fixed, or to discover anything new about myself. But I'm curious. I want to get out and continue exploring this world. But I'm a chancer. And whenever there is an obstacle in my way, it is in my nature to try to overcome it.*

Tomorrow, she'd sit down with Sean, explain what she needed to do, go over the details of the case, and find another avenue to pursue. And then she'd do it.

They couldn't continue their journey until this mystery was solved.

So now, more than ever, she was determined to solve it.

# CHAPTER SEVENTEEN

Mere seconds after Diana settled into bed, intending to write in her itinerary what she'd done all day, she rolled over and was awakened by a loud *thwack!*

She opened her eyes to bright morning sunlight. Peering over the edge of the bed, she saw her itinerary, spread spine-up on the dusty floor. Lifting it up, she stared at the open pages. The left one had her pledge: *On this trip, you must do something that scares you at least once a day.*

On the right, it said: *Pamplona. Since I've been here, I've r*

That was all. There was a long line of black ink down the page. Had she really been so tired that she'd nodded off in the middle of writing?

Probably. All she knew was that she'd had an incredibly good night's sleep. Thoughts of last night's resolution flooded her mind: *Whenever there is an obstacle in my way, it is in my nature to try to overcome it.*

And she was ready. She sprang up, ready to tackle the day.

She quickly grabbed her things and went out to the hallway, listening for the sounds of Sean's snoring, but she heard nothing. She showered and dressed, and when she went out to the kitchen, found him once again, reading the newspaper, two coffees on the table in front of him.

And, of course, a churro.

"How did you sleep?" she asked him. "That couch couldn't have been comfortable! Your whole body was hanging off of it."

"Oh, fine, fine. Good morning, love," he said, dipping the newspaper down. "I'm a little sore but I think it's more old age and not taking care of myself that did it. How are you? How did you sleep."

"Very good, thanks."

He let out a groan and folded the newspaper, then tossed it on the chair. "I have to say, without the excitement of the bull runs, there isn't much news to speak of in these parts."

"Oh?" she said, sitting down beside him and picking up the churro, smelling the sweet cinnamon sugar. "Thanks for this. You sure know the way to my heart."

He laughed. "Well, consider it a peace offering."

"A peace offering? For what?"

"For last night. For ridiculing the idea of going on a pilgrimage. It might not be my cup of tea, but it doesn't mean it wouldn't enlighten other people. If it's something you want to do, you should do it."

She shook her head. "Well, you're probably right. I kept thinking of this whole trip as a way to find something, prove something about myself, and you're right. It's silly. If I just make memories and enjoy the ride, that's enough. It should be enough."

He eyed her carefully. "But it's not, is it?"

She sighed. "I don't know. I feel like there should be more. Like I'm missing something. And part of it is that I hate not knowing things. De Leon's death—I want to find out what happened to him. I can't be this close to his murder and not want to know."

"And that will make you happy?"

"No. Probably not. But it'll make me free to go off on the next leg of this journey, at least, and right now, that's the best thing I can hope for." She smiled. "I'll worry about happiness later."

"All right. Then I agree. We should dig some more." He took a sip of his coffee. "What are you thinking?"

She wiped the sugar from her lips. "That's the problem! I'm not thinking anything. I really don't know where to go from here. Maybe if we just walk around a little more, something will come to me."

He nodded. "It's a plan. So, your ex-husband has a fiancé, eh?"

"Yes," she said with a shrug. She was surprised at how easily she could say it, considering the thought of Evan moving on had hurt her so much, before. Maybe it was because, more and more, she'd been seeing the cracks in the foundation of their relationship. No marriage was perfect, no matter what it looked like on the surface. "My ex-husband is having a second youth, I guess. Marrying a girl who's young enough to be his daughter. But it's okay."

"It is?"

"Oh, yes. I used to be bitter, but not anymore. She's a sweet girl. You know, she even asked me to give her away at the wedding. Turns out she doesn't really have a mother figure, and I know it's odd, but that's what she sees me as."

She'd hoped he'd say something about his past relationships, but he didn't. He simply said, "Ah, that's good of you."

She thought about asking him if he had an ex but chickened out. It seemed like something he didn't want to discuss. And maybe, she'd find out that he was already married, and had left his poor wife in Ireland to gallivant around Europe. So instead, she said, "It reminded me of De Leon and his young wife. It's funny how at first, we all suspect the worst. That she's marrying him for the money. That's what we all thought—that she was a nasty, money-grubbing gold-digger who'd gotten her claws into him. But the more I've gotten to know Tilda, the more I think we were wrong to believe that. I really do think she loves him."

"Yeah? What made you think so?"

"Well, she's a little immature, wanting the extravagant, white wedding, all the frills. But I don't think she's doing that because she wants to spend his money—she's just caught up in the wedding hoopla she sees on social media," Diana said. "But when I spoke to her just now, she sounded very sincere when she said she really loves him and will do anything for him. I believe her."

Sean said something in response, but at that point, Diana wasn't thinking. She was thinking back to Tilda, when she'd said, *I'll do anything for him.*

She wasn't thinking of her in relation to DeLeon's young wife, though. Now, she was thinking of Pablo Arroyo's wife. Was it odd that she'd tracked Diana down, trying to defend her husband? And that she'd been so adamant that he should not be a suspect?

"Wait," she said, interrupting Sean. "I just thought of something. What if Pablo Arroyo's wife was sick of the bickering between the two men, and she did it for him?"

Sean leaned forward. "I'm listening. Why would she do that?"

"Well, it just makes sense. Why else would she come to us, professing his innocence so loudly to everyone who would listen. She could've easily gotten to the corral because her husband owned bulls there. No one would question it. Maybe she was sick of De Leon, picked the lock hoping it would point to someone outside, and let the bull run? And when her plan backfired and suspicion still fell upon her husband, she had to do something to try to take the blame off of him?"

Sean stroked his chin. "Could be. You want to go and talk to her?"

Diana nodded. "It's the best we have to go on right now."

He clapped his hands together. "All right. I'm ready. Let's go ahead and do it."

She stood up. "Great. Let me—"

"Wait." He stopped and looked around, a little panicked, so that Diana thought there was something seriously wrong. Then he reached over onto the chair and pulled out his horned hat, fastening in on his head. "Okay, now I'm ready."

She rolled her eyes.

# CHAPTER EIGHTEEN

Moments later, they were standing in front of the modest row home belonging to Pablo and Mercedes Arroyo.

"You know, love, she's not going to be very happy if you accuse her. She came to you before, for help," Sean murmured.

"I know that. I'm not going to outright accuse her," she said, climbing the steps. "I was planning on being more subtle than that. Besides, I don't know if she came to us for help . . . or to throw people off her trail."

She knocked on the door, and a moment later, Mercedes Arroyo answered, holding a watering can, looking worried. She sighed with relief when she saw Diana. "Oh, thank goodness. I thought it was them. The police, and that terrible detective."

"No, just us," Diana said sweetly. "We just wanted to see if you had any more developments. Can we come in?"

She nodded and let them in, to the same kitchen they'd been in before. As they sat down, she said, "Would you like some tea?"

Diana shook her head and waited for Sean to say he wanted a beer. But this time, he didn't, maybe because he was worried that Diana was about to say something insulting, that would get them thrown out. "So the police have been back here?"

She nodded and stood on her tip-toes to water a few hanging plants in the sun-filled window of the kitchen. "Again and again. They might as well set up a post outside our house. They keep asking questions. Especially after Pablo showed them the scratches on the lock." She sighed. "Now I ask you . . . Why would he show that to them, if he was guilty?"

Sean said, "Well, it's something they would've figured out on their own, the first time they searched the corral."

"True. But he's been very forthcoming. If he was guilty, he might have changed out the lock or something. He's been cooperating with all their requests."

"Requests, like what?" Diana asked.

"They want to check the corral. They want to search our house. They want to see his office. He let them see everything. The only thing he say no to was going inside *El Gordo's* stall. He say no to that. That make them suspicious," she said with a shrug.

"Why did he say no to that?"

"I told you. Because he knows what *El Gordo* can do, and he wants no more blood on his hands."

"I see," Diana said. "But refusing to just makes him look more guilty."

"He's saving lives! That's just the kind of honorable man Pablo is. He's very good. It couldn't have been him."

"But who else could it have been?" Sean asked. "It had to have been someone who regularly went into the corral, someone whose presence there wouldn't raise any suspicion."

Diana nodded. "Did you go there a lot?"

"Yes," Mercedes said, now watering a small herb garden on the windowsill. "Often, I came to bring him his lunch."

She stopped and swung her head toward Diana suddenly.

"Wait . . . you're not insinuating *I* had anything to do with this?"

Sean winced and buried his face in his hands.

"No," Diana started. "What I mean is—"

"*Dios!* I came to you for *help*," she said, clearly hurt. She pointed to the cross over the door, then crossed herself. "I am a good Catholic! How could you think I would do such a thing?"

"Well, no, I—"

"I was nowhere near the corral, either! I told you that I saw De Leon at the bullring. That is *blocks* from the corral!"

"Yes, you saw us there, too, but the fact is that the police pointed out to me that you can get to the corral from that place in minutes. So that really doesn't exonerate anyone, unfortunatel—"

"But I went to the market! That's where I was going, when I saw you both. I needed to go to the fish market to get the shrimp for my *paella*. I always make paella the first day of the festival. It's a tradition. You can ask anyone. And even though the race was going on at the time, plenty of people saw me at the market. Believe it or not, many people don't like the run. I don't. I never watch it. Too bloody." She swallowed, and her face turned dark. "It gives me bad memories."

"Bad memories?" Diana asked, confused.

The woman reached down and lifted her long skirt. There, on her lower calf, was a massive scar, in shades of angry red and purple. The raised, mottled skin told the tale of a horrific injury. "This was what I got from *El Gordo,* the first night my husband brought him home."

Diana gasped.

"Yes. It was a little over a year ago. I used to be a fixture around the corrals, back then, feeding the animals, talking to them. I liked the bulls. In fact, that was how Pablo and I met—my father was also a bull owner, and Pablo was his protégé, who took over his business. Everyone knew me there, but the bulls especially. They loved me. I took care of them." She shook her head. "*El Gordo,* from the moment I saw him, I knew there was something different about him. He looked at me as if he wanted to kill me. I thought he just needed time, so I gave it to him. And he did get better. Eventually, I thought he was like all the others. It was a mistake."

Diana scooted to the edge of her chair. "What happened?"

"I dropped a bucket into his corral and reached in to get it. *El Gordo* charge me, lifting me up so that my body fell into the corral. They he tried to impale me with his horns." She shuddered. "There was no mistake about it. He wanted to kill me. He wants to kill everyone."

Diana nodded. "So I noticed. I'm sorry that happened to you."

Mercedes shrugged and dropped her skirt over her leg. "I am over it, now."

"What I don't understand is, why didn't your husband do away with the animal, if it almost killed you?" Sean asked.

"The animal is very valuable. Even now that he's killed a person, the mayor won't let anyone touch him. He's a celebrity. Pablo talks about selling him, but if he did, the bull would probably wind up killing other people. And he doesn't want that to happen."

"Oh, my," Diana breathed.

"And as you can probably imagine . . . I am terrified of that animal. I have nightmares about it all the time. I would never have let it go free. I don't even go to the corrals anymore, at all . . . and I can't even watch the festivities, either. I suppose you can say that bull ruined it all for me."

Diana nodded, remembering her own nightmare about *El Gordo*. "I'm so sorry. But it does make me wonder who would let the bull go free. It had to be someone very brave."

"A little foolish too," Sean agreed.

"If someone did have a score to settle with De Leon, they could've found an easier way to kill him, for sure," she said with a shake of the head.

"That's why I think it had to be one of the other matadors," Sean said. Diana and Mercedes turned to him, considering it, as he added, "It has to be. No one else would be that crazy, would they?"

"But why?" Mercedes asked.

He shrugged. "Jealousy."

"I don't think so. All they had to do was wait for him to retire. He said he was going to, soon. Everyone knew that."

Diana blinked. That was what De Leon's wife had said, also, but his manager had said that it was not true. Was it odd that his manager didn't know that his own client was planning on retiring? "Who told you that?"

"I don't know." Her brow wrinkled. "It's been going around the grapevine. Pablo must've told me."

Diana exchanged looks with Sean. He looked suspicious, too. He must've thought the same thing. *Someone has been lying to us.*

"Well, thank you for speaking with us," Diana said, standing. "If I hear anything else at all, I will be sure to let you know."

"Thank you," she said, walking them to the door. "I appreciate that. Pablo and I want to know how this happened more than anyone else. I promise you."

Diana could see the sincerity in the woman's eyes, and for the moment, she felt guilty for even thinking she could've been the murderer. But as she said goodbye and stepped outside, she had her direction again, and a good idea of where she needed to go.

"What are you thinking, macushla?" Sean asked as she took the first steps and he struggled to keep up with her.

"The bullring. You're right when you said the killer has to be a matador, and where else would we find one of those?"

# CHAPTER NINETEEN

Once again, the streets were crowded with people taking part in the festival, but it seemed a bit less active today. Diana reasoned it was probably because after the Running of the Bulls and bullfights were cancelled for the remainder of the celebration, some people had just decided to go home.

Or . . . maybe it had to do with the massive black clouds, heading their way.

"Looks like a bad storm is coming down the way," Sean said to her breathlessly. The wind was picking up, sending leaves blowing, vendors scrambling to gather their goods before they got lost on a gust. "Glad I have my trusty hat to keep the raindrops out of my eyes."

"Right. Faster," she urged him, just as lightning slit the sky, followed by a huge bang of thunder. A fat drop of rain fell on her shoe. "Uh-oh."

The bullring was in sight. There were no protesters there, but there were several people, gathered outside to pay homage to Alfredo De Leon with flowers and crosses, who went scrambling for shelter. Diana skidded to a stop when she saw the police officer from earlier, standing outside, guarding the place. She looked around, trying to determine what to do.

"Don't tell me you're going to try to get back in that place," Sean whispered to her as another raindrop fell on her cheek. "You might have been able to fool them once, but—"

"But you're going to help me, this time."

He glared at her. "I don't like the sound of that."

She smiled, the words, *On this trip, you must do something that scares you at least once a day,* ringing through her head. This would qualify. In fact, it was downright dangerous.

"Sure, you do. All you have to do is create a commotion so I can get past that police officer and inside the door."

He lifted an eyebrow. "What kind of commotion?"

She patted his shoulder. "You're a creative man. I am sure you will think of something."

He eyed her doubtfully but shrugged. She decided that was as good as an agreement to the plan. "I'm just going to walk over that way. When I give you the signal, you go. Got it?"

He gave her a half-hearted thumbs-up.

"You can do it!" she whispered over her shoulder to him as she headed for the side of the arena, away from the entrance. If she could get to the wall without the police officer seeing her, once Sean created the distraction, she reasoned she should easily be able to slip in behind her. Picking up her pace, she crossed the cobblestone street and got into position, about ten yards away from the back entrance she'd used the day prior, then turned to Sean, who was standing on the street corner.

She nodded at him to go ahead.

At once, he dropped to his knees and let out an agonizing wail.

It was so loud, everyone around turned to look at him. It even drowned out the rumble of thunder overhead. It was so convincing, too, that for a moment, Diana could only stand there and stare at him, wondering if he was okay.

"They took it from me!" he shouted. "It's gone!"

Most people probably thought he was just another crazy. With that hat, he had to have a couple screws loose. The police officer watched him for a moment, and then jogged over to him.

Diana would've loved to see more of the performance, but she had work to do. Tearing her eyes away from it, she rushed to the door and pulled it open, then slipped inside.

It was much darker inside now than it had been yesterday. When her eyes adjusted to the minimal light, she skirted along the edge of the wall, wondering if anyone was there at all. She listened at the first room, the locker room, and hearing nothing, peeked inside. It was dark.

Stepping inside, she found herself in utter darkness, since there were no windows. She felt at the wall and found a light switch. Immediately, the room was cast in bright fluorescent light. Scanning the room, she found all the normal items of any men's locker room—rows of lockers, tile walls, benches, sinks, and showers.

She walked deeper into the room, unsure of what she was looking for. Some of the lockers had padlocks on them. She opened one that wasn't locked, and found, as she anticipated, an empty space. Then she turned to a bulletin board on the wall, which had pictures of a few matadors and old, yellowing news clips of some of the fights. One was of De Leon, proudly holding a bloody bull's ear over his head, teeth bared, a look of fierce victory on his face.

Thunder boomed overhead, making her jump. Letting out a shaky breath, she crept deeper into the locker room, peering behind a wall. All she found were a series of dripping showers and toilet stalls, and a janitor's closet.

Sighing, she was just about to leave when she noticed another door, on the other side of the room. It was closed, and unmarked, behind a laundry bin, full of used towels.

Skirting around it, she pushed the door open, finding a small hallway. In the hallway were several closed doors, each with a piece of tape on it, and a name. Some of them had posters and pictures of bullfights on them, and news clippings with headlines about the matador's bravest kills. She read each one, stopping when she came to the one that said, *Alfredo De Leon.*

*These are the dressing rooms for the famous matadors,* she realized, trying the doorknob. Unfortunately, it was not only locked; it had yellow police tape over it. *Of course they're locked, dummy. You think a famous matador would just leave his door open for anyone to go in?*

Interestingly enough, his door had no photographs or newsprint on it. She wondered if it had been removed by the police.

Ready to give up, she turned around and leaned against the cinderblock wall, wondering what else she could do. That was when she spotted the door behind her. That one was for De Leon's friend, Luis Castrovilla. She remembered briefly what the young matador had said. *"I've been fighting for eight years. Killed four-hundred bulls in my time, or more. I lost count."*

On a whim, she reached over and tried the doorknob.

Surprisingly, it opened.

She stood there for a few seconds, blinking in disbelief. The crack of light that shone in from the hallway illuminated what looked like a massage table and a few chairs.

A loud drumming sound started overhead, echoing the mad beating of her heart. Diana realized that it was the rain, pounding the rooftop. Pushing the door open wider, she took one glance back toward the entrance, and confirming no one was there, crept inside, holding her breath the entire time.

She felt for the light switch and, finding none, tripped over a pile of shoes and clothing as she made her way to the desk and pulled the chain for a banker's-style lamp on a small corner desk. Then she looked around, finding an armoire filled with shiny, sequined matador outfits and hats. There was also a large, wall-sized poster of Luis, standing regally in the center of the ring, charming the bull with his cape.

At his desk was a mirror, the frame of which was filled with mementos—photographs with famous fans, postcards from admirers, dried flowers. There was also a picture of a busty young girl in a bikini, with the words, *Te Amo, Luis! – Vi* scribbled on it in black sharpie. As she looked closer, she found several more of them, love notes, written to Luis. Of course, he was a rock star—he had plenty of admirers.

She opened a drawer and found a pile of letters, all folded. Picking through them half-heartedly, she sighed. How was learning about Luis' love life going to help her catch Alfredo De Leon's killer?

Then she pulled out a letter that was different. It wasn't written on pink or pretty stationery—it was a typewritten note on ordinary white letter paper. Diana could see that much because the typing had bled through the thin stock. As she unfolded it, she saw a regular business letter, addressed to:

*De Leon—*

It was in Spanish, but using an app on her phone, she was able to translate a word: *Engaña.*

*Cheat.*

She scanned down the letter and saw the last sentence: *ultima vez.*

She knew what that meant: *Last time.*

There were also a lot of capitalized words and exclamation points. Whoever had written this was clearly passionate.

She was no expert, but this looked an awful like an extortion letter.

It was signed by someone named *J.P.*

*This is evidence. Evidence that De Leon was being blackmailed. He must've told Luis about it before he died,* she thought. *And because it wasn't in De Leon's possession, the police never found it.*

She folded it back up again and tucked it in her pocket. She'd bring it to the police. Or . . . first, she'd talk to Sean about it. He could at least translate it a little better than she had, to make sure it was what she thought it was.

She dug around in the drawer, looking for anything else that might help, but there were only love letters from fans and photographs of scantily clad women. She reached inside and pulled out a pair of lace . . . underwear?

Wincing, she dropped it quickly and was just about to slam the drawer shut in disgust when she heard the unmistakable sound of a door creaking open. Then, a male voice called out. *"Hola, ¿hay alguien aqui?"*

Diana froze, looking around frantically. She heard footsteps, but because of the echo through the tiled room, couldn't tell if they were getting closer. Straightening, she inched closer to the door, tucking herself behind it. The squeaking sound of wheels mingled with the footsteps, then there was the sound of a faucet being turned and running water.

She moved in such a way that she could peer through the crack from behind the door, and down the hallway, toward the main locker area. There, she saw an older man in a baseball cap and dark t-shirt, tattoos up and down his arms, walking among the lockers. He stooped to pick up something on the ground, and then started to whistle out of tune.

A janitor. She watched as he sauntered behind the wall, toward the janitor's closet. There was the sound of the door opening, and more water running. It sounded like he was filling a bucket to wash the floors.

*I have time,* Diana thought, squeezing out from behind the door.

She stepped cautiously into the hallway and toward the main locker area. She was just about to squeeze around the laundry bin and make a mad dash for the door when the faucet turned off and the footsteps resumed. Now, there was no question. They were coming closer.

*Not good,* Diana thought, scanning the area around her. She wouldn't be able to reach the door without being noticed. *Definitely not good.*

A second later, she saw the shadow of the man, stepping around the corner, and without a second thought, dove head-first into the laundry bin.

# CHAPTER TWENTY

The smell of sweat, mold, and baby powder mingled together sourly in her nostrils as she burrowed under the damp towels, piling some of them over her head. Once she'd done that, she listened, heart in her throat, as the whistling got louder.

*This is the dumbest thing you've ever done, Diana,* she thought to herself miserably as she tried not to gag at the smell of the moldy towels. *You could've just gone to the door and pretended you went in the wrong room. But now, if he finds you here, you're in serious trouble!*

Curled up in fetal position in the center of the bin, trying hard to breathe through the small opening she'd created for herself, she heard the sound of a mop slapping against the tile floor. Great. So he was going to be cleaning the entire floor. This would take a while.

Only a moment later, though, her back started to hurt and she wondered if she'd be able to stay this way, this long. *I'm too old to be doing this stuff,* she thought, reaching around to massage her lower back.

Suddenly, a door creaked open, and another voice said, "*¿has visto a un intruso?*"

*Intruso.* Intruder? Were they looking for her?

The janitor said "No," but then the other individual began asking him additional questions. Diana ventured a peek over the rim of the bin. It was the officer from outside, along with what looked like a security guard from the bullring.

So apparently, Sean's distraction hadn't lasted long. She wondered where he was and wished desperately that she could magically transport herself over there.

"*Ven aquí,*" the security guard demanded.

And then, to Diana's relief, the three of them filed out of the locker room.

Diana let out the breath she'd been holding and quickly scrambled out of the bin. Opening the door only a fraction of an inch, she peered out to find the hallway empty. She rushed down the hallway, the way she'd come, and slipped out the door, undetected. When she was outside, the rainstorm had dissolved to a thin drizzle. Once she was far enough away from the bullring to not arouse suspicion, she stood there for a moment, letting the rain fall on her face and thanking the heavens that she was free.

"You look like that bloke in *The Shawshank Redemption,*" a voice said behind her.

She jumped, and then realized it was Sean, leaning against a lamp post, watching her. "Oh my gosh," she said, grabbing at her chest. "Don't give me any more heart attacks today. I've had enough."

He chuckled. "Sorry my distraction didn't last as long as I'd have liked. Speaking of heart attacks, they didn't buy mine."

Diana's nose wrinkled. "I thought from what I saw, you were pretending that you'd had something stolen?"

"Oh, yes, I did. At first. I told them I'd had my bag of souvenir stolen. But then she started to call someone to come take me down to the police station to file a report, so I fell to my knees and told them I was having a heart attack."

Diana couldn't help but be impressed at the lengths he'd gone to. "Really?"

"Really. Only they called for an ambulance, and it came right away. I've got to hand it to Pamplona, their emergency crew is top notch. But the last thing I wanted them to do is strap me to a machine and cart me away, so I 'recovered,'" he made air-quotes as he spoke the word, "And told them it must've been a panic attack over all the stress."

She looked around, making sure that they were alone. "I can't believe they bought that. And I can't believe you *did* that."

He grinned. "Just like I can't believe you've snuck into the bullring. Twice. What happened to you. Why does your hair look like that?"

She smoothed her hair down, finding it a tousled mess, even under the weight of the drizzle. The rain was picking up, so she pulled him toward a store overhang on the opposite corner of the street. There, she said, "I ended up under some towels."

"Towels?"

"Not important. But I found something. I think. I couldn't really translate it that well." She reached into the pocket of her jacket and pulled out the paper. Unfolding it, she held it in front of him. He read it, eyes narrowing. "What does it say?"

"It says, '*De Leon. You think you have so much dirt on me? Don't forget, I have just as much on you. You have been cheating this industry for years and have cheated for the last time. You are a disgrace. Paying the organizer for that spot in the fight was disgusting! No one will forgive you for that. You see, not only do I know, but I have evidence!! I own you, De Leon. You tell anyone, forget ever retiring with honor... you'll never work in this town again. For the LAST time . . . Think twice!! Meet me at 8 AM sharp on C. De Los Muertos. J.P.'*"

He looked up, and for a moment, they just stared at each other in silence.

*Calle de Los Muertos.* Exactly where De Leon had been found dead. He'd been lured there.

"So the poor bloke was being blackmailed, eh? Where did you find this?"

"Right. I found it in a drawer in the locker room, among Luis Castrovilla's things. I think it proves . . ." She pointed to the bottom of the letter. "J. P. Juan Perez, De Leon's manager. That's why he said that he didn't know De Leon planned to retire. He was the only one who hadn't heard that, when as his manager, he should've been the *first* person De Leon told. Perez was forcing him to stay in the business. He wanted to meet him at the course."

Sean's eyes went wide. "You think that Perez was really responsible?"

"Well, think about it. We knew it had to be someone who wasn't afraid of *El Gordo*. Whose appearance at the corral wouldn't raise suspicion."

"But why was it in Luis Castrovilla's things? And why didn't he say anything?"

"Well, I was thinking about it, and it makes sense. Castrovilla was managed by Perez, too. De Leon had warned Castrovilla to stay away from Perez, but Castrovilla thought he had a good relationship with Perez and didn't want to get his manager in trouble. So he kept quiet about it."

Sean nodded. "Makes sense."

"You remember how Perez was, too. There was something oily about him. Something off. He didn't have much love for De Leon, but he did love the money he brought in. And of course Perez would *say* he was on the course, watching the event, near the bullring. I bet no one actually remembers him being there, though."

"You're probably right," he said, stroking his chin. "So you did it, *macushla.* You found the real killer. What do we do now? I think we should go to see what Mr. Perez has to say for himself."

"I agree," she said, with a smile. "Let's just make one small stop, first, to be absolutely sure."

Sean smiled and stepped aside. "All right. Lead the way."

*

Perez's office was only a block away, but unfortunately, when they got there, the place was locked up, a *CERRADO/CLOSED* sign hanging askew in the window. Frowning, Diana paced the area, wondering what to do.

"Maybe we should just go to the police . . ." Sean suggested.

She checked her phone. "It's not ten o'clock yet. Maybe he opens later? Let's just wait."

By then, the rain had stopped. They sat on the curb, even though it was wet, and Diana pulled out her phone. She had a message from Lily: *I just heard that you are going to give away Vidal at the wedding? Seriously?*

Diana sighed. "Vidal" was her daughters' name for their soon-to-be stepmother because she was all about her hair. Diana'd probably get an earful from both of her kids for that decision to walk her down the aisle. They both thought that their father marrying Tilda was a mistake, but the truth was, Diana had learned to rise above it. It was better to get along. So she typed in: *Yes. I think we all need to be a little nicer and respect your father's decision.*

As she pressed "send," Sean nudged her hard at her elbow. She looked up to see Perez, walking their way. The graying, slight man was wearing a shabby suit and had a pronounced limp she hadn't noticed before. He said, "Ah, my friends from yesterday. Are you waiting for me?"

"Yes, Señor Perez," she said, scrambling to her feet as the man fiddled with the key to the office. "Can we come in?"

"Of course. I doubt I'll have much to do considering all the bullfights in the area are still suspended. I should've gone on holiday," he said jovially, in a way that made him seem very pleasant. It almost hurt Diana to have to accuse him. But if he was guilty, and it seemed he was. . . at least of blackmail, which was nasty business . . . then she had to do it.

When they got inside, he pointed to the coffee maker in the corner of the office. "Would you like some? I could make a pot?"

"No," Diana said shortly, looking at Sean, who also seemed a little reluctant. Perez needed to stop being so *nice* to them, or else she'd never be able to confront him. "I just had a couple more questions for you about your relationship with Alfredo De Leon."

"Oh, yes. Come on in my office. You'll be more comfortable there."

By the time they sat down across the desk from him, Diana was ready to burst. She said, "I've come to find out that many people knew De Leon intended to retire. His wife, the Arroyos . . . it was common knowledge on the bullfighting grapevine. And yet you did not know? I find that very strange."

"Well," the man said pleasantly, lacing his fingers together in front of him. "He might have batted the idea around, but never seriously. He was flighty, prone to moods. He couldn't decide what to do from day to day. And bullfighting is not an easy business, so it's common for fighters to have crises of confidence."

"So he never came to you and announced plans to retire?"

"No. Of course not. If he'd been serious about it to others, I might be the last person he would tell, because he wouldn't want to disappoint me."

That made sense. Unfortunately. She gnawed on the inside of her cheek and finally took a deep breath. "How long had you been blackmailing De Leon to stay in bullfighting?"

He visibly stiffened. "What?"

"You knew he'd paid off some officials in order to get into certain fights. And you knew that if the world knew about it, his reputation would be ruined. So you held it over him, insisting that he stay in fighting and not retire. True?"

134

Perez swallowed. "That is ridiculous."

"But then De Leon decided he'd had enough of it and intended to out *you* for blackmailing him. And you knew that would ruin your reputation," Sean said. "So you let the bull loose that killed him, removed the barrier, and . . ."

"No!" His face now red, he stammered, "Well . . . all right. Yes. Alfredo did want to retire. And I was doing my best to convince him not to. I told him that if he left me, he'd never work in the town again. And I told him I'd make it difficult for him if he did. But I never intended to go through with any of that. And my God, I didn't *kill* him. That's for sure."

So he was just going to deny it? Diana decided she had no choice. She pulled out the letter and held it in front of him. "So where did this come from?"

He read it, confusion dawning on his face, giving way to indignation. "What . . . where did you get this?" When Diana didn't answer, he looked up. "I didn't write this. This is a sham! Someone's trying to frame me!"

"Who?" Sean asked.

His face went blank. "I don't know. Someone. De Leon had enemies, yes. But I had them, too. People were jealous of my success with bullfighters and wanted to take my business. That's what this is." He stood up and pointed to the door. "I want you out of here. Now. Both of you."

The two stood up in unison.

As they did, the front door opened, and the police swarmed in, Detective Carrera at the head. "Right on time," she said, smiling. It was a good idea that they'd stopped there, earlier, to inform Carrera of the letter they'd found. He'd agreed that the letter was evidence enough to take Perez in for questioning.

"We heard everything," Carrera said, motioning to his officers. "You're under arrest, Juan Perez."

# CHAPTER TWENTY ONE

After that, everything happened so quickly.

Flabbergasted but beaten, Perez stood and allowed them to snap the handcuffs onto his wrists. He shook his head as they led him away. "This is all wrong. I'm innocent. I'm telling you. I had nothing to do with De Leon's death."

"You'll have to take that up with the legal system," Carrera muttered as he was dragged out.

Carrera stopped in front of Diana, and for a moment, she thought he might thank her. Instead, he simply nodded, and continued on his way.

"I think that was his way of saying *much obliged,*" Sean said with a shrug, reaching out a hand to her to shake. "Good job, lieutenant."

She shook his hand, and together, they walked outside. "I can't believe that happened."

By the time they got to the sidewalk, the police cars were heading away, toward the station. "Well," he said, "It was all because of your remarkably daring sleuthing skills. You have a career in that, I think, if you want one. Ever fancy yourself a private detective?"

"No. I really couldn't have done it without your help. You and that ridiculous hat of yours."

He laughed and peeled the hat from his head, looking at it sheepishly. "That's right. You're a good sport. Most women would've stolen this hat and burned it by now."

"I actually think it makes you look quite a bit more dashing," she teased.

They walked along the street, to the front of the bullring.

"I wonder if they'll start up the bullfights again, now that they've caught the killer?"

He shrugged. "Well, even if they do, I don't want to see one."

"You don't? But you were so excited—"

"Yes, but you're right. It's violent business. I'm not sure I'm interested anymore." The walked a little farther, toward the festival, and he said, "Well, you are free, now. I suppose that means we can be on our way."

"You *always* could have been on your way, anytime you wanted to leave," she said to him. "But I appreciate you staying with me while I was stuck here."

"Ah, I couldn't abandon you. After all, I was the one who suggested you come on this crazy adventure."

She smiled. "You didn't force me into the Running of the Bulls."

"Oh, I just about did. And you behaved magnificently." They stopped at a corner, and he turned to her. Here they were, at a crossroads, and it felt like their relationship was at one, too. She looked up at him as he said, "You're quite a woman."

"Why, thank you," she said, her cheeks heating. She quickly added, "And you're quite a man. So did you have any idea about what comes next on this adventure? More tooling around Pamplona?"

He shook his head. "I think, personally, I've seen all I need to see of this town. What do you think?"

"I agree." It was funny how, every time she was cleared of a murder, she couldn't wait to leave town. It wasn't that the place had soured; it was just that she felt like she'd done everything she needed to do.

"I think one more night here ought to do it, and then it'll be time to head out. After all, the accommodations aren't ideal, thanks to me."

"They were fine," she told him honestly. They hadn't spent much time at all in the flat, anyway. "But yes, it will be nice to move on."

"It will be. Any thoughts as to where you want to go?"

She noticed that he hadn't said whether he'd be going with her. So maybe this was the end of their time together. Maybe he had other plans. He hadn't even spoken to her of his past life, except to say that he was in sales. Who knew? He might have had a family at home, a wife. Someone he was planning to spend his next stop with. "Well, I was thinking I might just do that pilgrimage. I might not discover myself, but it looked like it had very pretty scenery. And I could use the exercise."

He lifted an eyebrow. "Do you want company?"

Her eyes widened in surprise. "I thought—"

"I know what I said," he grumbled with a shrug. "But what can I say? It might be superstitious nonsense, but it does have lovely scenery.

And who knows, maybe it will prove me wrong, and I will learn something about myself I never knew."

"Really?"

"Yes, and I've always wanted to see that cathedral at Santiago de Compostela. I hear it is quite a sight."

"All right." She felt a shiver of excitement down her spine and found that she was more enthusiastic than ever about the idea of heading off on the trail. Not because she didn't believe she could do it alone, but because despite all of his eccentricities, she really liked Sean. She didn't want to have to say goodbye. At least, not yet. "That sounds great. But . . ."

"But?" he prompted. "Is something wrong, lass?"

"Well, I don't know. You tell me. You've never told me anything about your life, and I've been a little afraid to ask. You're very congenial, you like to talk and ask me questions, but you never say anything about yourself!"

Confusion flooded his eyes. "Ah . . . haven't I?"

"No! And I had to wonder. You said you've been puttering around Europe for months. You had to have left something behind? Do you have family? A life? Anything?"

He stared at her, his expression softening. "That's right. I suppose I haven't been very talkative about that. I apologize. It's not something that I talk about often."

"Oh, well, you don't have to—"

"No." He held up a hand. "I want you to know. It's only fair to you. I'd hate for you to think I'm not being honest with you, love, but it is a bit of a sordid tale."

She held her breath, waiting.

"My wife, Maggie, who gave me six children, now grown, died, six months ago," he said, his voice full of uncharacteristic seriousness. "It was very sudden. She was only fifty-five."

Diana brought a hand to her mouth. "Oh, my goodness. I'm sorry."

"When it happened, my kids were out of the house. They tried to take care of me, but they have their own families now. Maggie and I were very close. We spent every day of our lives saving up, because we planned to take a trip around Europe, one day. We never got there," he said. "She wouldn't have wanted me to sit around and mourn her. And so this is my way of doing exactly what she would've wanted for me."

Diana nodded, tears in her eyes. "I'm so sorry. But should I be on this trip with you, then, if—"

"I think you and Maggie would've gotten along. You two are very alike," he said with a sad smile. "You're a tad bit more tenacious than she is, solving those murders. But I like it, I do. And I'll be honest with you, the first few months of my travels, I couldn't bring myself to have fun. I was just going through the motions. But this time, with you? It's been fun. More fun than I knew I could have. And I think my Maggie would be happy to know you and I are having fun, together. That's all she'd want."

Diana took his hand. "I'm really glad to have met you. I was only going through a divorce, but I remember thinking I'd never be able to climb out from under it. Now, it doesn't seem so bad. And I think you had a lot to do with that."

As they stared into each other's eyes, all Diana could think about was her reason for making this trip in the first place. It hadn't been a voyage of finding something new about herself. Truth be told, it wasn't to find a lost love that she knew, deep down, she'd never meet again. It was to find an *old* part of herself. That fanciful girl she'd long-since buried, the one who believed in true love, the one who believe the world was hers to be conquered.

So when he leaned in to kiss her, she closed her eyes, and when his lips pressed against hers, she felt the same butterflies that had fluttered about wildly during her very first kiss.

It was a very nice feeling, indeed.

"So you are Catholic. Tell me," she said when they'd pulled apart. "What is the story of St. James? Why do people from all over make the pilgrimage to that cathedral?"

"His remains are supposedly buried there."

"And he's important?"

She was embarrassed that she knew nothing about religion at all, but Sean gave her an understanding pat on the hand. "He was one of the twelve apostles. Together with his brother John, they were the Sons of Thunder. He was the first of the apostles to be martyred for his beliefs. And he's the patron saint of Spain."

"Son of Thunder?"

He chuckled. "Had a bit of a temper, he did. Wanted Jesus to use the power of God to strike down their enemies."

"Hmm. That is nothing like Evan. He's agreeable to everything."

"And you?"

"Well, I'm agreeable to *some* things."

"And what do you say we go back to the flat and pack, and then go out on the town for one last fling in Pamplona?" he asked, holding out his arm to her.

She nodded. "I'm agreeable to that."

She looped her arm through his and they walked back to the flat, like two young, star-crossed lovers, to get ready for the next leg of their adventure together.

# CHAPTER TWENTY TWO

Sean held Diana's hand as they took a street away from the festival crowds, climbing up the crooked cobblestone street until they reached a small bistro in a wooded, residential area. Diana looked around, charmed by the tiny homes and shops, and the center square, complete with bubbling fountain. "This is so cute. I can't believe you've never been here before."

Sean grinned. "I have not, *macushla*. I promise. I asked Enrique to recommend to me the most romantic restaurant off the beaten path, and this place was his idea. So blame him if it's terrible."

The place was called *Casa Azul,* and it was, indeed, a Blue House, on the corner. It was the shade of the night sky, the windows blazing with yellow light. There were potted plants and flowers surrounding the place, and a white picket fence leading out to a garden, adorned with fairy lights. He led her inside, and the hostess took them upstairs to a balcony in the back of the house, overlooking the dimly lit garden.

It was definitely romantic, with a soft breeze blowing and soft instrumental music being piped in from inside. "Oh, this is lovely," she said, sitting and opening the menu.

"No octopus this time," Sean said with a wink.

"Then what will you get?"

He shrugged. "I have an idea. Since it's our last night in Pamplona, let's really go wild. Let's have them surprise us. Tell them to give us their best, whatever it is."

She laughed. After all she'd been through, she felt just brave enough to go ahead and do that. No questions. She closed her menu. "That sounds perfect."

He motioned to the waiter and ordered a bottle of red wine. Then he spoke in Spanish to the waiter, telling them just what they'd like to do. The waiter's eyes gleamed with excitement. He nodded, collected their menus, and headed off.

Sean leaned forward. "I think now we've done it. We're in for it."

"Oh, come on. After everything, I don't think I can be surprised by much," she said, placing the napkin on her lap. "Besides, I scanned the menu. It was in Spanish, but nothing looked too crazy. You'll probably have them give us the most expensive items on the menu."

He shrugged. "Ah, the *langosta.*"

"*Langosta?*"

"Lobster."

"I'm up for that," she said with a smile.

"Or I could go for some good steak." He licked his lips. "I tell you, I miss the meat and potatoes of home. So what do you think they're serving Juan Perez for dinner tonight in the jail?"

She shrugged. "Probably not lobster. But I don't feel right, making light of the situation. I don't know—he seemed so nice. Yes, he clearly didn't like De Leon. And yes, he was blackmailing him to stay in the business. But that might have been in desperation to keep his client. He didn't seem like a murderer."

"I suppose a lot of people don't seem like murderers," Sean pointed out. "Which is why, on all the news reports after the fact, they always interview a neighbor who says, *I never thought he was capable of such a thing.*"

"True. But he only admitted to the blackmailing. Not to the murder. What good would it do for him to murder De Leon? That's basically ensuring that he will never make him money again."

"You said it yourself. De Leon must've threatened to reveal what Perez was doing to the other matadors."

"I suppose that's true. And well, he had—" She stopped as the waiter approached with a plate of what looked like little sausages on crusty bread.

"This is our *txistorra pintxo*. Small bite. Our specialty," the man said in broken English. "A real treat."

"Oh, it looks delicious," Diana said as Sean reached over and picked one up.

"I'm famished," he said, shoving the entire round into his mouth. He chewed, his eyes lighting up, and said, mouth full, "Mmm. Good."

Diana tried a nibble of one. He was right. The sausage was spicier than the traditional breakfast sausage, and it was in some kind of tomato sauce that reminded her of a dish she'd had in Italy. "Wow. Love it."

"What were you saying about De Leon? Before? He had . . . what?" Sean asked, still chewing as he reached for another.

"Was I?" The thought had left her. She reached into her mind, trying to remember what it was. Just as it was about to come to her, her phone buzzed with a text, and the thought quickly flittered away as she looked at her phone. It was from Bea: *You really agreed to give Vidal away at the wedding? That's not fair. I was going to ask you to give me away!*

Diana sighed. What a way to put a damper on the mood. She almost silenced and put her phone away, but the urge to reply was too great. She put up a finger to Sean and texted: *What about your father?*

Her reply: *I want both of you to walk me down the aisle.*

Diana wished she could be there in person to help her youngest plan her wedding. It seemed like every day, there was a catastrophe. Diana couldn't remember ever having this much stress, planning her wedding to Evan. She typed in: *Well, the weddings are not the same day! I can do both.*

Immediately, Bea replied with: *But I wanted to be your first time.*

She laughed. Of all the silly things to worry about . . . *Honey, this time with Tilda won't be my first walk down the aisle. Don't worry, walking you down the aisle will be special because you're you.*

A moment later, she responded with: *Okay, Mommy. Love you. Hope you're having fun. Call me later.*

Diana looked up and found Sean staring at her with amusement on his face. "Sorry," she said. "You have six kids. How do you not have them constantly texting you, every minute of the day, wanting advice?"

He chuckled. "Maggie was the one with the sage advice. I was the one with the jokes. So they know better than to come to me for wisdom. You must be very smart for them to constantly be wanting yours. What was it, now?"

"Oh, my youngest. She's in Japan and planning a wedding, and it's a new disaster every second."

"Ah, I remember that time."

"Your children are married?"

"All of them."

"You have grandchildren?"

He nodded and reached into his wallet, pulling out a giant roll of pictures. "Sixteen of them."

"Sixteen!" She admired all the photographs, each of smiling faces that slightly resembled Sean's. "Wow, they're beautiful children."

"Yes. These photos are old, though. They're quite a bit older now. But all under the age of twelve."

"Are they all in Ireland?"

He shook his head. "No. My oldest, Greg, is in Kilkenny, with his wife and the triplets. They're four, and a right good handful. I sat for them, now and again. I love children. Keep you young, you know? But the rest are all over Europe, actually. France, Portugal . . ."

Her jaw dropped. "So you were visiting them?"

"Yes. That's part of the purpose of my trip. But the reason I came to Barcelona was because I met a pretty lass in France, and I couldn't stop thinking about her."

She blushed and looked away, unable to keep the smile off her face. "You did."

"*Shah,* of course," he said with a smile. "Do you still have the coin?"

She reached into her purse and pulled out the old, worn coin with the Gaelic runes upon it. He'd given it to her, and she'd flipped it a few times to decide where to go on her travels. "I do. It's my good luck charm."

"It was mine too."

"Oh! Did you want it back?"

She held it out to him, but he took her hand and closed her fingers over it. "No, what I mean is, it led me to you. Unexpectedly. And I couldn't be happier."

She smiled, blushing hard and hot, and looked out upon the garden, cast by the fairy lights and the moon's glow in a dim blue light. She said, "Well, I think of all the places you've taken me, this is my favorite."

"Mine, too."

They were still holding hands across the table when the waiter appeared with two bowls. He set one in front of each of them and said, *"Estofado de toro.* Another specialty of ours. You like."

Diana took a fork and stabbed at the chunks of meat, swimming in a brown sauce. It looked like the traditional beef stew she used to make every Sunday for her family at home. As she picked up the first forkful, it hit her. *"De toro?* So is this—"

"Bull stew," Sean said, already chewing. "I know you said you were quite done with bulls, but I don't think you'll mind them like this. It's quite delicious."

She took a taste and nodded. "You're right. They're much easier to stomach when they can't breathe down your neck."

They both laughed.

Sean said, "So what was it that you were saying before, about Alfredo De Leon? You shouldn't worry about that Juan Perez character. You have the right man. He was afraid of losing his business because De Leon was planning on outing him to the other matadors as a blackmailer."

"Well, now he's really lost his business. That's for sure. His business and his freedom. I bet he'll go to jail for a long time. It was a very risky thing for him to do, considering. But I suppose he had to have been so angry at De Leon for not listening to him that he just snapped . . . went to the corral, unleashed the bull . . . then ran to the other part of the course and pushed away the barrier . . ."

Diana trailed off, remembering something that had happened earlier that day.

"That's odd."

"The whole case was odd, from beginning to end, if you ask me." Sean tilted his head. He'd already polished off his stew, and here, Diana had only taken a single bite. She sat there, her fork full of the next bite and halfway suspended between the plate and her mouth, but the more she thought about it, the more doubtful she became.

"No, what's really odd is that Juan Perez had a limp. I saw it when he was coming toward us on the street. He was so *slow*."

Sean's eyes narrowed, as he seemed to follow her train of thought. "So you think . . ."

"How could he have let that bull go, and then run all the way to the other side of the course to open the barrier so he could've gotten through?"

Sean shrugged. "It wasn't that far. Besides, there was no saying how much time passed from the time the bull was let out of its pen to the time the first gunshot went off. It was possible it was in the corral with the other bulls, waiting, and no one noticed that it shouldn't have been there. During that time, he could've gotten to the other side of the course."

"But I think people would have had to have noticed. It was *El Gordo*. Everyone said you can't mistake him."

"I see," he said, draining his glass.

He pointed to her stew, urging her to eat up, when she remembered what she was going to tell him, before. "Oh, and what I was saying before was that I guess De Leon was already in the process of telling other matadors what Juan Perez was up to. Because I found that letter in Luis Castrovilla's dressing room."

"You did?"

She nodded. "So I guess he showed it to him. But I don't really understand why Castrovilla had that letter and didn't tell anyone . . ."

She froze as the realization hit her at full speed. Luis Castrovilla was a good matador, but everyone said De Leon was better. He was young and spry and capable of handling a bull, any bull. He had a reason to want De Leon out of the way, and if he was around the corral, it was likely no one would've noticed. And the letter . . .

"Oh, my gosh," she breathed, as it suddenly came to her. "That's the reason Luis Castrovilla had the letter in his possession."

"I'm sorry, what?" Sean asked in confusion. "What's bothering you?"

"Don't you see? De Leon didn't show that letter to Luis to give him evidence that he was being blackmailed. I mean, maybe De Leon did tell Castrovilla that he was being blackmailed to stay in bullfighting. And Luis, sick of the fact that he was always going to be number two, took matters into his own hands. *He* wrote that letter. And then he took it from De Leon, once *El Gordo* had killed him."

"You're saying that . . . Luis Castrovilla murdered Alfredo De Leon and was trying to frame their manager for the crime . . ." Sean said, understanding finally dawning. "Now, that's diabolical."

"It just makes more sense. But I don't have any proof," she said, tapping her fingers on the table thoughtfully. "But I think I know how we could find out."

Sean looked down at her plate. "Don't you want to finish your stew?"

She threw her napkin on the table and pushed away from it. "I don't think we have any time. Can we get the check? I think we might have put an innocent man behind bars!"

# CHAPTER TWENTY THREE

Unfortunately, Casa Azul was in the opposite direction of the bullring, on the other side of the festival, so Diana found herself running as she made her way through the crowded streets. Drunken revelers were out in full force, enjoying the warm summer night. She wove around them, until finally, the ring came into sight.

Stopping at the corner to catch her breath, she looked around and realized she was alone.

"Sean?" she asked, peering over the crowds in the darkness.

A moment later, he broke through, panting. "Here. My God, love. Now I see how you were able to outrun that bull. You have some moves on you."

The only move she was concerned about now was the one that she'd performed earlier, where she'd gotten a potentially innocent man arrested. The guilt overwhelming her, she marched across the street, toward the bullring. This time, it was dark, but there were no security guards or police officers standing by. They'd probably decided that since the case was closed, it wasn't necessary anymore.

"You're going to sneak in there for a third time, aren't you?" he asked, struggling to keep up with her.

She shrugged. "What else can I do?"

"You could call the police."

"No, because I don't know for sure. And I don't want to be wrong twice. But I *have* to know," she said. "If we can just get into this locker room again, I bet we might be able to find some other evidence. He had a pile of other notes and things there. I just didn't go through it all because I thought that letter was the smoking gun. But I bet if I can just get in there . . ."

She went to the back door, and, looking around as she'd done before, pulled on it.

But it was locked.

She pulled again, as if that would magically produce a different result, but again, she was disappointed. "Oh, no."

Sean shrugged. "Well, if you're not interested in the front door, I guess we could call it a night."

She wrinkled her nose. "You don't really think they'd leave the front door wide open, if this one is closed. Would they?"

He shrugged. It was worth a try. She walked around to the front, checking in the darkness for anyone who might be watching them. But the police and security had their hands full with whatever was going on in the festival. She reached the front double doors and casually pulled on one of them.

It opened.

"There! I told you!" Sean said triumphantly as she shushed him and slipped inside. She'd never been to this part of the ring before, and it was so dark in there, lit only by moonlight streaming through the doors, that she had to squint to see what was there. It looked like a lobby, similar to that of a movie theater, with posters of famous matadors and their kills on the walls. Once her eyes adjusted, she noticed the lobby restrooms, and the box office.

Creeping past that, she froze when she heard a noise, deep inside.

She looked at Sean. "Did you hear th—"

It came again, closer.

Then, footsteps. There was no doubt about it. Someone was coming. "Hide!" she whispered, rushing for the ladies' room. Behind her, Sean must've had a different idea, because he hurried off in a different direction. She reached the restroom and pushed on the door.

It didn't budge.

It was locked.

She shoved it one last time when a figure came around the corner nearest her. He took a step back and let out a gasp of shock. Then he said, "*Qué estás haciendo aquí?*"

Straining to see in the darkness, she noticed right away the handsome face of the man she'd spoken to yesterday. It was Luis Castrovilla, in the flesh. He was dressed in a warm-up suit and had a duffel bag slung over his shoulder.

"Oh, Mr. Castrovilla!" she said, every inch of her skin prickling with goosebumps. Was she in the presence of a killer? "It's me, Diana St. James."

His eyes narrowed. She saw no recognition in them whatsoever. "Who?"

"I spoke to you yesterday, out in the ring?"

"Oh, right. Were you from press?"

"Uh . . ." She couldn't remember what lies she'd told, if any, to get him to talk. Right now, she couldn't think of anything other than that he could've killed Alfredo De Leon. And maybe it was time for the truth. "No. What are you doing here? Training?"

He smirked. "That's right. My training's never done. What are *you* doing here?"

"Oh, I . . ." She looked around. "When I was here yesterday, I used the restroom. And I think I left my phone in there. I came here to check, but the door's locked. I guess I need to call security?"

*So much for the truth.*

He shook his head. "Don't bother security. This is no problem. It's a good thing you ran into me. Lucky for you, that kind of thing's my specialty," he said, motioning her back. He reached into his pocket and pulled out what looked like a Swiss Army Knife. Pulling the file out, he scratched the metal panel a bit before sticking it inside the keyhole. He turned it around a bit until there was an audible click, and then the door sprang open. "Easy."

Meanwhile, Diana had been staring at him, wondering if that was just the way he'd let the bull out of its pen. When he grinned at her, she quickly replaced her shocked expression with one of delight. "Oh, wow. You did that so well. Thank you. Looks live you've done that before."

She cringed when his eyes found her in the dark. "Yeah. I have."

She took the door from him and pushed it open the rest of the way, wondering what she should do. The safe thing, she reasoned, would be to let him go, and call the police later, explaining what she'd learned.

Yes, that was the plan.

She stepped in, flipped on the light, and turned to find him standing there. She expected that he'd have left, but he seemed to be waiting for something. "Well, again, thank you."

"But, *por favor, Señora,* I need to lock up after I go. The ring shouldn't have been open to spectators. So I will need to wait until you've gone," he said.

"Oh." Bristling, she turned away, toward the empty restroom. Was he on to her? There was something about his tone that didn't seem quite right.

He was on to her.

Teeth chattering in her skull, she walked up and down among the stalls, looking for her "phone," while trying to calm herself down so she could face Luis Castrovilla again. She went to the mirror and looked at herself, trying to gauge if her expression gave her away.

Finally, when she knew she'd taken too long, she plastered a smile on her face and turned to the door. Opening it, she sighed. "Oh, well. Looks like it isn't in there."

He was leaning against the box office window. "A shame, really."

Suddenly, the phone in her purse buzzed with a text.

His eyes immediately went to it. She froze. Then she smiled. "Well, I've got to be on my way. Maybe I'll call tomorrow for the lost and found! But thanks!"

She tried to step around him, but he sidestepped in front of her, blocking her way. With sudden force, he grabbed her bag, unzipping it, then pulled out her phone, much to her chagrin. "Well, look at that. I found your phone," he said, dropping her bag and holding it up. "So, Diana St. James. Who are you, exactly? And what the hell do you want?"

She reached forward to grab it, but he held it high, out of reach. "I wanted to know why you killed Alfredo De Leon."

He laughed. "Don't be stupid. He was killed by accident."

Shuddering, she did her best to keep her voice even. "No. Someone let that bull out. Someone moved the barrier. Someone who wanted him dead. You."

He backed away, then pocketed her phone, ensuring she'd never be able to call the police. Luis said, "You're insane. How'd you work that one out?"

Diana looked around, desperately, for Sean. But he was nowhere in sight. "I didn't know it for sure. Not until I saw you jimmy that lock. That's how you let *El Gordo* out. You knew Alfredo was being blackmailed. He told you as a warning, but you saw an opportunity. You wrote that letter, pretending to be his manager, saying that you wanted to meet him. You lured him out to *Calle De Los Muertos*. You let the bull loose and opened the barrier. Didn't you?"

150

The indignation on his face melted away, leaving a smug smile. "Alfredo De Leon was a piece of garbage. Always bragging, always saying how much better he was than all of us. I was sick of it. Every other matador in town should be thanking me for what I did. They all wanted to do the same. I guarantee it."

Diana gasped. "So you killed him?"

"Yes. I'll admit it. I did, and I'd do it again."

He advanced toward her. She braced herself against a wall, trying to get away from him, looking around frantically for escape. *Maybe I should've planned this a little better, before I went around accusing him.* Where was Sean? He reached a hand out to her, and she batted it away. "What are you doing? We need to go to the police—"

"Police? Are you kidding me? You don't think I'm going to let you leave here, now," he said, his hands out, ready to wrap around her neck.

She let out a squeal, and before she could, a dark blur descended upon them, knocking Luis off his feet. Diana had only a split second to process what was happening in front of her—Sean, coming to the rescue by shoving Luis to the floor—before he grabbed her arm and said, "Come on, let's go!"

He tried to pull her toward the lobby doors, but Luis was in the way, and already climbing to his feet, a look of murder in his eyes. She let out a sharp cry as he dove for them, narrowly missing them as they charged into the darkness of the bullring.

Luis was at an advantage. As someone who considered the ring a second home, he knew all the hiding places. Sean, however, stumbled through the almost pitch-blackness of the hallway, reaching for doors and trying to pull them open. He stopped at one, yanking on it, the growled, "Locked."

Diana, heart beating hard, looked behind her. She couldn't see him, but she could hear the sound of footsteps coming closer. "Where do we—"

He dragged her to another door, then another, trying each one in vain. They were all locked. Finally, they came to a set of double doors that opened. "Thank God," she breathed as Sean nudged her inside.

But as she looked around and saw the moonlight, reflecting off the risers, she realized she wasn't inside. She was outside, in the giant ring. Above, the stars shone, but around her, everything was blackness. She took a few tentative steps, then broke into a run, toward the center of the ring, her feet sinking into the soft earth.

When she reached the place where the arena opened up into the vast oval-shaped field, she looked around, wondering what to do. Sean came up behind her. "Did you call the police?" she asked him.

He nodded. "Let's go that way. We'll hide in the bleachers until the police come."

"Okay," she said, following him toward the risers. He had a head start, so he made it there before she did, taking the steps two at a time. As she reached the bottom of the stairs and was about to climb, the door swung open, and Luis began to barrel straight for her.

Changing her direction, she ran out, into the middle of the ring, all the while, feeling the echoing sound of his footfalls in the earth, getting closer. Now, there was nowhere to hide. She was out in the open. She raced across, to the barrier on the opposite side, where she could go no farther.

When she spun around, she saw Sean, on the opposite side of the ring, waving and shouting, trying to get Luis's attention. But Luis was focused on one thing. Her.

"You're a meddling little witch, aren't you? You and your little boyfriend?" he snarled, creeping toward her.

For a moment, she felt like she had when she'd been cornered by *El Gordo*. Luis had the same, rabid look in his eye, something that said there was no telling what he would to do her. All she knew was that he wouldn't stop until she was dead.

In fact, strangely, he almost *sounded* like *El Gordo*. She could've sworn he let out an animal snort that sounded very much like the bull before he'd charged her.

"You'd better stop," she said, her voice shaking. "The police are on their way."

He shook his head. "And you'd better stop meddling where you don't belong."

He took a step forward.

There it was again. The snort of a bull. And then, the clanging of something hard, against metal. That *wasn't* Luis. It was coming from somewhere beside her. Turning her head to the side, she saw it. That angry bull. *El Gordo.* He was there, in a cage, thrashing his horns about wildly.

That gave her an idea. "You're in trouble. If you stop now, it won't be so bad. It's only going to get worse," she said. Keeping her back against the wall, she inched sideways, toward the corral.

He laughed. "You don't get it. He screwed with my life. He deserved to die. Everyone knows it."

Sean had climbed down the steps and was now heading toward her. But he wouldn't be there in time. She reached the side of the gate at glanced over at it. Sure enough, it wasn't a padlock. All she needed to do was lift the lever, and the gate would open.

It all happened in a blur. He lunged forward. As he did, Diana tore off toward the side, releasing the lever on the gate. *El Gordo* exploded out like a rocket fired from a cannon, bucking and jumping wildly, throwing clouds of dust into the air.

For a split second, Diana felt sure that he'd attack *her*, his favorite target. But then he set his eyes on Luis Castrovilla, dressed all in red, and a new target was acquired. The bull charged at full speed.

Gone was the typical grandiose performer's air that matadors usually displayed in the ring. At this unexpected development, Luis let out a yelp and turned on his heel, running for the exit.

Before he could reach it, though, the floodlights turned on, and security swarmed in through the doors. Luis hesitated, for the briefest of moments, but it was long enough for *El Gordo* to catch up with him. *El Gordo* bowed his head, digging at Luis with his horns, lifting him up, balancing him in mid-air like a skilled juggler while he wailed, before tossing him into the stands.

Behind her, loud clapping and cheers rang out. She turned, stunned, to find Sean and several members of the police force, applauding the show from the risers, where they'd gone to escape the mad bull. Sean wolf-whistled and shouted at her, "*Olé!* Take a bow! Should we cut off his ear?"

Her heart still beating hard in her chest, she managed a smile and a demure curtsey. "Honestly? Now, I think I *really* have had enough of this bull stuff."

# CHAPTER TWENTY FOUR

"I was always the best! Always! You should give me a medal for what I did!"

Those were the rantings of Luis Castrovilla as he was lifted off the floor, disheveled and beaten from his run-in with *El Gordo,* and placed under arrest.

Yawning, Diana leaned against Sean as they watched the former second-best matador in Pamplona escorted out of the ring, with both his ego and his body bruised. It felt nice to have a man's arm around her, especially now, when she couldn't stop shivering.

She'd said in her itinerary, *On this trip, you will do one thing every day that scares you.*

To that, she had to say, *Just one?* During these past few days, she'd experienced enough scares to last a lifetime. Now, she wouldn't have minded a nice, easy lounge chair near a pool, with a tropical drink and a good book. Her heart probably couldn't take much more of this.

"So," Detective Carrera said, sidling over to her with a frown that almost, but not quite, seemed to be bordering on a smile. "You were wrong."

"Hey," Sean said in her defense. "She might have had the wrong bloke at first, but she got it right in the end. Near risked her life, trying to bring him to justice. I'd say you owe her a big debt of gratitude."

Diana smiled gratefully at Sean, but the detective ignored him. "How did you work it out that Castrovilla was the real killer?"

"Well, the letter. I realized that if Luis had had something like that in his possession and De Leon had shown it to him as proof that he was being blackmailed, if Luis was truly innocent, he would've wanted the killer to be found and would've given it to you. But he hadn't. I found that suspicious. And when we came back there, and he opened the lock on the ladies' room with no trouble, I realized he'd have no trouble opening the lock on *El Gordo's* pen."

Sean nodded. "Right brilliant, I'd say. If you didn't have her, you'd still be fishing around the festival for clues."

Diana blushed. His effusive praise was going to swell her ego. She held up a hand to tell him to cut it out. "You're going to let Juan Perez out, right?"

"He still has to answer for the blackmailing he was doing," Carrera said, running a hand coolly through his salt and pepper hair. "A few more matadors came forward and said he's been doing it to them, too. So we're not done with him."

"But you're done with me, right?" she asked hopefully.

He nodded. "Truthfully, I don't mind if I never see you again."

She shook his hand. "I'd be insulted, but the feeling is mutual. I'm going to have bull nightmares for a long time after this, I'm sure."

"Goodbye, Ms. St. James," he said, nodding at her and Sean, and heading off to join the other officers.

"Goodbye," she said, and turned to Sean. "Ready to leave this place?"

"More than ready. I think we have a date with the Way of St. James, tomorrow."

*

Early that morning, Diana and Sean headed out to the closest shopping district and found backpacks and hiking boots for their trip. They easily transferred all of their luggage into the bags, strapped on their heavy-duty hiking boots, and got ready for the first leg of the trip, hiking out of Pamplona.

"I can't wait," Diana said, and for the first time, she really meant it. During this trip, there'd been a lot of nervous apprehension. But now, she was full of excited anticipation. Maybe it was having Sean with her, or maybe it was just that she was on The Way of St. James, knowing exactly where she needed to go.

"Me neither, love," he said, as the two of them headed down the stairs to say goodbye to Enrique. They found him behind the cash register. He filled jugs of fresh water for them to sip along the route.

Then he came around the counter and gave Sean a big hug. "I hope that you enjoy your pilgrimage, but you do not stay away too long," he said, then looked at Diana. "I will leave you with the immortal words of

Rumi: 'It is your road, and yours alone. Others may walk with you, but no one can walk it for you.' Enjoy!"

She hugged him, too. "Thank you. I will remember that."

When they stepped outside, it was late in the morning, and it was warm, but not hot, with a slight cool breeze in the air. Diana took a deep breath as she dug her thumbs under the straps of her backpack. It was perfect hiking weather.

They took a single step—just one—and Sean's phone began to ring.

Stopping, he lifted it out of his pocket and checked the display, his brow tenting. "It's my son in Kilkenny." He held up a finger and answered. "Hello, Colin, my boy, how are you?"

Diana meandered a bit away, not wanting to intrude on the conversation. She stepped forward, wondering where they'd stop for the first night. Where the adventure would lead them. What things they would see and experience. A thrill overcame her, and she shivered in the shade of the market.

"All right, see you then," Sean said, ending the call. When he turned around, he was frowning.

She could tell from the look in his eyes that something was wrong. "Is everything okay?"

He shook his head. "Turns out, my boy Colin's wife, Angela, was in a car accident."

Diana gasped. "Is she okay?"

"Yes, fine, really. Minor injuries. But she has a bit of whiplash, and he really could use me to come and help with the triplets while he goes off on his business trip." He looked at his backpack and sighed. "I'm afraid I have to catch a flight back to Dublin right away."

"Oh, of course," she said, sympathetic. "I understand completely."

He smiled sadly. "Do you? I know how much this trip meant to you."

She nodded. "Please, don't worry about me. I have family, too, remember? If it was me, I'd be taking the first flight back home, no questions. You should go."

He took her hand and patted it. "You're very understanding."

She forced a smile. The last thing he needed to see was how disappointed she truly was. She was right here, and the beginning of the path she felt she was *made* to take, and now, she could go no further. Or could she?

*It is my road, and my road alone.*

"I'm only sorry you won't be able to make the voyage with me. It would have been fun. I've enjoyed being with you. I just didn't want it to end. But I do understand, Sean. Really."

He studied her. "You're going to go it alone, then?"

She shrugged. "Well, I don't have any other plans."

He pulled off his backpack and set it down on the sidewalk. She could see from the way his brow furrowed that there were so many new thoughts churning in his head—likely, all the plans he needed to change in order to catch that flight to Dublin.

So he surprised her when he grabbed her hand, and said, "Then come with me."

"What?" Her mouth hung open.

"You heard me. I have enjoyed being with you, too. More than I thought possible. And I don't want it to end, either. So why don't you come with me, love? We can visit my family in Kilkenny, tool around Ballygangargin, and I'll show you the sights of my little village."

She would've thought it was a joke, since Sean was given to joking. But his eyes glimmered with complete sincerity, so much so that it knocked the breath right out of her. She swallowed. "I'm sorry. You just shocked me. This is so sudden."

"I know it is. I know it is, dear. You told me you didn't want any more surprises on your vacation, and here I've gone and popped another one on you." He shrugged. "But what can I say. It's one of the good kinds of surprises, right?"

She nodded. "Oh, yes."

"And the truth is, I don't understand it. But I've been around the block quite a few times and I've never felt like this. Like I don't want to give things up with you, right now. I know in my bones when things feel right. And this feels right."

It did feel right. And it felt wrong to just separate, so easily, after what they had shared. But she'd spent so many sleepless nights, thinking about this European trip. And jetting off to live with a romantic interest while he took care of his grandkids wasn't on her itinerary.

No, she hadn't been following her itinerary very well at all, but it was supposed to include seeing new places. Enjoying new cultures and food and landmarks. Not this.

"I . . . I can't," she finally announced. "I'm sorry."

His smile fell. "Oh. Why not?"

"I have a list, I've created," she said, pulling out her itinerary. "It used to be filled with landmarks and places I needed to go. But now it's my bucket list of things I want to do."

He looked at it as she flipped the pages. There were dozens of things she'd done: unexpected things, like *be moved to tears by beautiful music,* which had happened unexpectedly at the train station in Austria, when a little boy played his violin for her on the platform. Wonderful things, like *Fall in love with Italy.* And then of course, there was her pledge to *Do something that scares you, once a day.*

But so many pages that had been unfilled, so many pages needed to have adventures written upon them, accounts of new bucket list items to cross off. The more she looked at those empty pages, the sadder she felt. It felt like her journey was only half-done.

"And I haven't done nearly enough. I'm only a couple months into my year-long trip. I have so many things I need to--"

"But you have time, love. You're young. You have years ahead of you."

She shook her head. "I may have thought that once. But things have changed, and now . . ."

"Life is about taking advantage of the opportunities that are presented to you. Not about marking things off on a silly list—"

"It's not silly," she snapped, defensive.

He seemed to recoil, realizing that he'd said something wrong. "I didn't mean that. What I meant is . . ." He trailed off, then lifted his phone. "It's all right love. I'm sorry that I sprang that on you like that. You shouldn't have to change everything for me. It's not fair for me to expect you to."

She nodded with relief.

"But I'd love it if you did." He winked. "I'll just call the airline and see how quick I can get a flight back."

He turned away from her and made the phone call, while she stood there, alternating between gazing wistfully at the path on the Way of St. James, and watching his back. She had a feeling whatever she chose in the next few moments would affect her life forever.

*I hate choices like this,* she thought bitterly to herself.

But she'd made the life-changing decision to quit her job, to take this flight, even though everyone in her life had told her it was madness. And yet, she was still here. She hadn't returned home in shame, ruing the day she ever made that choice. Sure, crazy things had happened, but she was better off, now. She wouldn't have changed it for the world.

No matter what she chose, she would be okay.

He turned to her, suddenly, still speaking into the phone. "The earliest flight you can get me is tonight? All right. If that's the best you can do, fine. Book me on it."

Then he looked at Diana. "One ticket or two?"

# CHAPTER TWENTY FIVE

The road was comprised of rolling countryside and farmsteads, and a rather even elevation. Not too tough a walk, though it was about twenty kilometers. Easier, in fact, than she'd expected. Diana patted her leg, just imagining what this kind of walking would do for her glutes, as she took a shortcut through sun-drenched farmland.

She broke through a field of sunflowers and made it into the village of Puente la Reina at around dinnertime. She wasn't hungry, though; she'd been snacking on some ripe grapes she'd picked along the walk, the entire time, which had helped to quench her thirst.

*Oh, yes. This is the life. Beautiful scenery. Beautiful day. Only my own thoughts to keep me company. Could anything be better?*

She grabbed a blade of long grass from the side of the road and, just like Rachel Hawkins had done before her, began to braid it.

*It's so quiet. So peaceful. This is my road, and my road alone. I'm so glad I get to experience it with my favorite person. Myself!* she thought, flicking away the braided grass and pulling out her guidebook. As she did, the gorgeous medieval stone bridge came into view.

She looked up from her guidebook and smiled as she crossed the narrow pilgrim's bridge, *Bridge of the Queen,* as the city was named for, over the still water. The sun was beginning to slip in the sky, so when she turned around to see how far she'd come, she saw a long shadow of herself, helplessly alone, on the path behind her.

*Nope, Diana. Don't think that. You made the right choice. This is the path of your dreams.*

She'd seen no one on the trip, so she'd mostly been in her head, wondering, again and again, if she'd made the right choice by leaving Sean behind.

*Of course you made the right choice. You said you'd do one thing each day that scared you. And this is scary. But totally right. The path has your name on it, after all!*

As she walked, though, her skin prickled, and her mind whirled with doubts. She thought about what he'd said to her. He'd kissed her lightly and said, "Well, if this is where we part, I hope to see you again. May you be held in the palm of His hand."

Now, as she clutched the Gaelic coin in her hand, she wondered why she hadn't tossed it to make the decision. After all, it hadn't led her astray before.

Standing at a corner, she decided to, after the fact. She tossed it up in the air, caught it, slapped it against her hand, and whispered, "Heads, I'm on the right path."

It was tails.

"Best two out of three," she said, tossing it again.

Again, tails.

"Traitor."

It glinted in the sunlight, mocking her.

Groaning, she shoved the coin in her pocket and pulled out her phone. She was hoping for a text from Sean, saying he couldn't live without her and was following her on the trail, but she knew that was fantasy. His family came first, and she wouldn't have liked him so much if it didn't. Instead, she had a message from Lily: *Where are you now?*

She texted back: *Just taking a solo hike. Leaving Pamplona now.*

A moment later, Lily came back with: *Mom, that's dangerous! You don't know who else can be on that trail! You shouldn't do that alone.*

Everyone was so worried about her, but she'd made it just fine, on her own. And she would, in the future. Of course, before, she'd been alone because she was forced to be.

Now, she was alone by choice.

Or did she choose that?

Pocketing her phone, she continued on through the village, admiring the narrow cobblestone paths and gothic Roman walls, churches and buildings. There, she came to a church. *La Iglesia de Santiago.*

No, it wasn't the famous Cathedral of Santiago de Compostela that Sean had wanted to see, but it did have her name on it. And it was pretty, in a Romanesque style, with an intricately carved portal. She climbed the steps and tugged on the massive wooden door. It opened.

Inside, she passed through the narthex and peered into the main area of the church. She peeked into the church, at the high vaulted ceilings, the triforium and clerestory windows, the gilded apse. One thing she'd learned from her architecture classes was that these churches didn't have many windows, so it was dark, but beautiful, nonetheless.

And yet, though it had her name on it, it gave her very little satisfaction. So she had to wonder, if the same would be true when she reached her destination's end? That cathedral was something Sean wanted to see, but, she realized, if she was going to see it for the first time, she wanted to see it *with him.*

*Stop it,* she told herself as she stepped out of the church. *You will see him again. It was never about the cathedral of St. James. It was about what you'd find on the journey. That's what you care about. Filling up your itinerary with all your adventures.*

She crossed the street to the hostel she was planning to stay at and stood outside it. The place was austere, no frills, like all of the hostels on the route. Still, it couldn't be much worse than the place she stayed at in Pamplona. And yet . . . that had been fun, regardless.

*Don't think about it, Diana.*

Reminding herself there was plenty of adventure to be had, up ahead, she squared her shoulders. She'd get a room and then go out for a bite to eat. Maybe she'd even meet some other people taking the journey, too, and make some friends. Yes, that would be great.

But the second she stepped inside the lobby and looked at all the other travelers, who all seemed to be in groups of two or more, her stomach sank. There were a few elderly couples, too, milling about the lobby.

*How lucky they are to be able to experience this all, together,* Diana thought. *Sure, it might be my journey, and only I can take it, but there's nothing wrong with wanting to take it with someone who I have fun with.*

And being in that crate-filled, musty old flat with Sean, even though he was quite the snorer, had been one of the best times she'd had.

Going out to eat with him and sampling all the foods she'd never thought she'd try was fun.

Running with the Bulls? As scary as the prospect was, that had been fun, too.

She'd done a lot of things she never imagined she'd do, since taking off from JFK six weeks prior. But the reality of it was, Sean had pushed her even further out of her comfort zone. He didn't think she was too old for any of it, and around him, she felt younger. He'd given her the courage to make this trip absolutely extraordinary. That's why, when she looked back, she had to admit, Pamplona had been her favorite stop on the trip, so far. He'd made it that way.

He was right. Something about it did feel right, between them.

And she didn't want it to end, either. Sure, he said he hoped he'd see her again, but Stephane had said that same thing, too. Now, here she was, still filled with regrets over something that had happened decades ago. Even now, the weight of it tugged at her, making her feel sick.

She didn't want that to happen again.

She *couldn't* let it happen again.

And it wasn't too late. For anything. New experiences, a new romance, new possibilities . . . it was all still there, waiting for her. She just had to know when to jump and grab ahold of it.

*"¿Necesita ayuda?"* the smiling clerk behind the desk said.

She shook her head and took a step backwards, toward the door. "I think I am in the wrong place."

When she escaped out into the hot summer's day, she *knew* she was in the wrong place. And she knew just what to do about it.

She grabbed her phone and placed the call. "Hello, do you have a flight leaving tonight from Pamplona, for Dublin? I'd like one ticket, please."

# CHAPTER TWENTY SIX

Diana managed to hail a cab to take her back to Pamplona. As the taxi pulled through the narrow streets, she drummed her hands on her thighs anxiously. Everything seemed to be going in slow motion.

When she'd left Sean, outside the market, he'd told her that he was going to spend time catching up with Enrique before heading off to the airport. So she had the taxi drop her off at the market.

She paid and jumped out, almost before the cab had come to a complete stop. Navigating around shoppers, she rushed to the front counter, looking for Sean. She saw Enrique working the register, but Sean was nowhere to be found. Had he left?

Enrique's eyes lit up when he saw her. He stopped mid-transaction and came over to her. "Diana! I am so happy! You came back!"

She nodded. "Where is Sean?"

"He will be happy you came back, too. He said he felt terrible to let you go."

Diana smiled. "But where is he?"

His brow wrinkled. "He took a taxi to the airport a half-hour ago. Flight leaves soon, yes?"

"Oh, no!" she said, turning toward the storefront window just in time to see the yellow taxi, speeding away. She covered her mouth with her hands. "I should've gone directly to the airport. How far away is it? Will I even have time to get there?"

"Not far," he said, snapping his fingers at the boy stocking the shelves nearby. He said something in Spanish to the boy, who nodded. Then he reached into his pocket and pulled out a set of keys. "Come. I drive you. You have plane ticket?"

"You will? That's wonderful!" she exclaimed, following him outside to a tiny blue sportscar.

He took her backpack and threw it into the back seat, and she climbed into the front passenger seat. He pulled away from the curb so fast, she barely had time to buckle her seatbelt. As he cruised down the street, going airborne over a dip, he said, "Sean will be happy. So happy. All he did was talk about you."

"Really?" she smiled, even as her heart sped up. If she missed the airplane, after this, she'd be so angry with herself . . . she'd probably want to do nothing more than turn around and take a plane back to the States.

"Oh, yes. Sean is my very good friend. I would like to see him happy. After his poor wife . . . he deserves to be happy."

"He is a very special man," she agreed.

When he pulled up at the airport, her nerves were wound tight. She jumped out of the cab and Enrique helped her with her bag, then gave her a hug. He said, "And don't forget—"

"I know, I know. *It's my road alone . . .*"

He shook his head. "I was going to say this—your feet have a way of taking you where your heart is."

"Yes," she said, throwing her heavy backpack over her shoulder. "Thank you. I won't forget that."

"Good! *Te deseo que tengas un buen viaje. ¡Nos vemos pronto!* Safe travels!"

Waving to him, she rushed into the airport, hoping security wasn't too busy. Luckily, she made it through in record time, then raced to the gate. Skidding to a stop when it came into view, she breathed a sigh of relief. The plane was still boarding, and there were a few people still lined up, waiting to go into the plane. No Sean, though. Maybe he was already on the plane.

Breathless, she approached the flight attendant, who scanned the ticket on her phone. "*Gracias.*"

When she got halfway down the ramp, a new worry gripped her: What if Sean didn't want her there? What if he'd changed his mind? What if he'd befriended some other woman while waiting to board the plane?

She checked her ticket. 14 B. She swallowed and held her breath when she entered the plan and turned toward the rows of people, already seated. The flight was packed, it seemed, not an empty seat to be found.

Scanning the faces of the people already seated, her eyes caught on the one familiar person on the plane. He was sitting at a window seat, staring out the window, a few rows back from her own seat.

Her heart skipped a beat as she approached. She leaned into the person sitting next to him and said, "Would you mind if we switch seats? I'm just two ahead, right there."

The man nodded. "Of course."

As the man stood up and began to shuffle into the aisle in the limited space, someone helped Diana put her backpack in the overhead compartment. When she finished stuffing it up there, she looked down at Sean to find him smiling at her.

"Ah, love, so you couldn't keep away, huh?"

"That's right," she said, sliding into the seat and sitting beside him.

"Well, I'm delighted, to say the least," he said, putting a hand on her knee and giving her a gentle squeeze. "Why did you give up the Way of St. James? I feel terrible."

"I didn't give it up!" she said, smiling to show him just how happy she was over the choice. She wasn't sad, not at all. "I just thought it wasn't the right time. I feel like it'd be a lot more fun if I did it with someone else. Someone who could tell me all about the cathedral when I got there."

"Well, that would be me," he said with a chuckle. "You'll have to put it on that itinerary of yours, then. You still have it, right?"

She pulled it out and looked at what she had written there: *On this trip, you must do something that scares you at least once a day.*

Then she crossed it out and wrote: *Just let your feet take you where your heart is.*

She went to put her phone on Airplane mode and saw a text from Lily: *Mom, that's dangerous! You don't know who else can be on that trail! You shouldn't do that alone.*

She wrote back: *Change in plans. I'm not hiking anymore. I'm on a plane, as we speak.*

Lily replied with: *Ok? So what's next on your itinerary?*

She looked down at the little booklet and smiled. Then she reached down and tore the thing in two. After all, who cared? There was no place she *had* to be. Nothing she *had* to do. The only thing she *had* to do was be kind to others, follow her happiness, and let everything else work itself out on its own.

And right then, at that moment, she was *so* happy.

Grinning, Sean took her hand, and kissed her knuckles.

It wasn't her feet taking there, but a plane. But it was all the same. She was leading with her heart. And she couldn't wait to find out where it was going to take her next.

# ALSO NOW AVAILABLE!

## MURDER (AND BAKLAVA)
## (A European Voyage Cozy Mystery—Book 1)

"When you think that life cannot get better, Blake Pierce comes up with another masterpiece of thriller and mystery! This book is full of twists, and the end brings a surprising revelation. Strongly recommended for the permanent library of any reader who enjoys a very well-written thriller."
--Books and Movie Reviews (re *Almost Gone*)

MURDER (AND BAKLAVA) is the debut novel in a charming new cozy mystery series by #1 bestselling author Blake Pierce, whose *Once Gone* has over 1,500 five-star reviews.

When London Rose, 33, is proposed to by her long-time boyfriend, she realizes she is facing a stable, predictable, pre-determined (and passionless) life. She freaks out and runs the other way—accepting instead a job across the Atlantic, as a tour-guide on a high-end European cruise line that travels through a country a day. London is searching for a more romantic, unscripted and exciting life that she feels sure exists out there somewhere.

London is elated: the European river towns are small, historic and charming. She gets to see a new port every night, gets to sample an endless array of new cuisine and meet a stream of interesting people. It is a traveler's dream, and it is anything but predictable.

But when a wealthy, high-maintenance passenger suddenly turns up dead outside of Budapest, the cruise has become a bit too unpredictable. Even worse: as the last person to see her alive, suspicion falls on London, leaving her no choice but to solve the crime (with her new sidekick, an orphaned dog), and save her cruise line and herself.

Laugh-out-loud funny, romantic, endearing, rife with new sights, culture and food, MURDER (AND BAKLAVA) offers a fun and suspenseful trip through the heart of Europe, anchored in an intriguing mystery that will keep you on the edge of your seat and guessing until the very last page.

Book #2 (DEATH AND APPLE STRUDEL) and book #3 (CRIME AND LAGER) in the series are now also available.

## Blake Pierce

Blake Pierce is the USA Today bestselling author of the RILEY PAGE mystery series, which includes seventeen books. Blake Pierce is also the author of the MACKENZIE WHITE mystery series, comprising fourteen books; of the AVERY BLACK mystery series, comprising six books; of the KERI LOCKE mystery series, comprising five books; of the MAKING OF RILEY PAIGE mystery series, comprising six books; of the KATE WISE mystery series, comprising seven books; of the CHLOE FINE psychological suspense mystery, comprising six books; of the JESSE HUNT psychological suspense thriller series, comprising nineteen books; of the AU PAIR psychological suspense thriller series, comprising three books; of the ZOE PRIME mystery series, comprising six books; of the ADELE SHARP mystery series, comprising thirteen books, of the EUROPEAN VOYAGE cozy mystery series, comprising six books (and counting); of the new LAURA FROST FBI suspense thriller, comprising four books (and counting); of the new ELLA DARK FBI suspense thriller, comprising six books (and counting); of the A YEAR IN EUROPE cozy mystery series, comprising nine books, of the AVA GOLD mystery series, comprising three books (and counting); and of the RACHEL GIFT mystery series, comprising three books (and counting).

An avid reader and lifelong fan of the mystery and thriller genres, Blake loves to hear from you, so please feel free to visit www.blakepierceauthor.com to learn more and stay in touch.

# BOOKS BY BLAKE PIERCE

## RACHEL GIFT MYSTERY SERIES
HER LAST WISH (Book #1)
HER LAST CHANCE (Book #2)
HER LAST HOPE (Book #3)

## AVA GOLD MYSTERY SERIES
CITY OF PREY (Book #1)
CITY OF FEAR (Book #2)
CITY OF BONES (Book #3)

## A YEAR IN EUROPE
A MURDER IN PARIS (Book #1)
DEATH IN FLORENCE (Book #2)
VENGEANCE IN VIENNA (Book #3)
A FATALITY IN SPAIN (Book #4)
SCANDAL IN LONDON (Book #5)
AN IMPOSTOR IN DUBLIN (Book #6)
SEDUCTION IN BORDEAUX (Book #7)
JEALOUSY IN SWITZERLAND (Book #8)
A DEBACLE IN PRAGUE (Book #9)

## ELLA DARK FBI SUSPENSE THRILLER
GIRL, ALONE (Book #1)
GIRL, TAKEN (Book #2)
GIRL, HUNTED (Book #3)
GIRL, SILENCED (Book #4)
GIRL, VANISHED (Book 5)
GIRL ERASED (Book #6)

## LAURA FROST FBI SUSPENSE THRILLER
ALREADY GONE (Book #1)
ALREADY SEEN (Book #2)
ALREADY TRAPPED (Book #3)
ALREADY MISSING (Book #4)
ALREADY DEAD (Book #5)

**EUROPEAN VOYAGE COZY MYSTERY SERIES**
MURDER (AND BAKLAVA) (Book #1)
DEATH (AND APPLE STRUDEL) (Book #2)
CRIME (AND LAGER) (Book #3)
MISFORTUNE (AND GOUDA) (Book #4)
CALAMITY (AND A DANISH) (Book #5)
MAYHEM (AND HERRING) (Book #6)

**ADELE SHARP MYSTERY SERIES**
LEFT TO DIE (Book #1)
LEFT TO RUN (Book #2)
LEFT TO HIDE (Book #3)
LEFT TO KILL (Book #4)
LEFT TO MURDER (Book #5)
LEFT TO ENVY (Book #6)
LEFT TO LAPSE (Book #7)
LEFT TO VANISH (Book #8)
LEFT TO HUNT (Book #9)
LEFT TO FEAR (Book #10)
LEFT TO PREY (Book #11)
LEFT TO LURE (Book #12)
LEFT TO CRAVE (Book #13)

**THE AU PAIR SERIES**
ALMOST GONE (Book#1)
ALMOST LOST (Book #2)
ALMOST DEAD (Book #3)

**ZOE PRIME MYSTERY SERIES**
FACE OF DEATH (Book#1)
FACE OF MURDER (Book #2)
FACE OF FEAR (Book #3)
FACE OF MADNESS (Book #4)
FACE OF FURY (Book #5)
FACE OF DARKNESS (Book #6)

**A JESSIE HUNT PSYCHOLOGICAL SUSPENSE SERIES**

THE PERFECT WIFE (Book #1)
THE PERFECT BLOCK (Book #2)
THE PERFECT HOUSE (Book #3)
THE PERFECT SMILE (Book #4)
THE PERFECT LIE (Book #5)
THE PERFECT LOOK (Book #6)
THE PERFECT AFFAIR (Book #7)
THE PERFECT ALIBI (Book #8)
THE PERFECT NEIGHBOR (Book #9)
THE PERFECT DISGUISE (Book #10)
THE PERFECT SECRET (Book #11)
THE PERFECT FAÇADE (Book #12)
THE PERFECT IMPRESSION (Book #13)
THE PERFECT DECEIT (Book #14)
THE PERFECT MISTRESS (Book #15)
THE PERFECT IMAGE (Book #16)
THE PERFECT VEIL (Book #17)
THE PERFECT INDISCRETION (Book #18)
THE PERFECT RUMOR (Book #19)

**CHLOE FINE PSYCHOLOGICAL SUSPENSE SERIES**
NEXT DOOR (Book #1)
A NEIGHBOR'S LIE (Book #2)
CUL DE SAC (Book #3)
SILENT NEIGHBOR (Book #4)
HOMECOMING (Book #5)
TINTED WINDOWS (Book #6)

**KATE WISE MYSTERY SERIES**
IF SHE KNEW (Book #1)
IF SHE SAW (Book #2)
IF SHE RAN (Book #3)
IF SHE HID (Book #4)
IF SHE FLED (Book #5)
IF SHE FEARED (Book #6)
IF SHE HEARD (Book #7)

**THE MAKING OF RILEY PAIGE SERIES**

WATCHING (Book #1)
WAITING (Book #2)
LURING (Book #3)
TAKING (Book #4)
STALKING (Book #5)
KILLING (Book #6)

**RILEY PAIGE MYSTERY SERIES**
ONCE GONE (Book #1)
ONCE TAKEN (Book #2)
ONCE CRAVED (Book #3)
ONCE LURED (Book #4)
ONCE HUNTED (Book #5)
ONCE PINED (Book #6)
ONCE FORSAKEN (Book #7)
ONCE COLD (Book #8)
ONCE STALKED (Book #9)
ONCE LOST (Book #10)
ONCE BURIED (Book #11)
ONCE BOUND (Book #12)
ONCE TRAPPED (Book #13)
ONCE DORMANT (Book #14)
ONCE SHUNNED (Book #15)
ONCE MISSED (Book #16)
ONCE CHOSEN (Book #17)

**MACKENZIE WHITE MYSTERY SERIES**
BEFORE HE KILLS (Book #1)
BEFORE HE SEES (Book #2)
BEFORE HE COVETS (Book #3)
BEFORE HE TAKES (Book #4)
BEFORE HE NEEDS (Book #5)
BEFORE HE FEELS (Book #6)
BEFORE HE SINS (Book #7)
BEFORE HE HUNTS (Book #8)
BEFORE HE PREYS (Book #9)
BEFORE HE LONGS (Book #10)
BEFORE HE LAPSES (Book #11)

BEFORE HE ENVIES (Book #12)
BEFORE HE STALKS (Book #13)
BEFORE HE HARMS (Book #14)

**AVERY BLACK MYSTERY SERIES**
CAUSE TO KILL (Book #1)
CAUSE TO RUN (Book #2)
CAUSE TO HIDE (Book #3)
CAUSE TO FEAR (Book #4)
CAUSE TO SAVE (Book #5)
CAUSE TO DREAD (Book #6)

**KERI LOCKE MYSTERY SERIES**
A TRACE OF DEATH (Book #1)
A TRACE OF MURDER (Book #2)
A TRACE OF VICE (Book #3)
A TRACE OF CRIME (Book #4)
A TRACE OF HOPE (Book #5)

Made in the USA
Monee, IL
13 August 2024